Printed and Published in Great Britain by D. C. THOMSON & CO., LTD.,
185 Fleet Street, London EC4A 2HS.
© D. C. THOMSON & CO., LTD., 2004.
ISBN 0 85116 846 9

(Certain stories do not appear exactly as originally published.)

'Fifties Fun-Folk

BASH STREET KIDS	SHAGGY DOGGY
ROGER THE DODGER	JONAH
GINGER'S SUPER JEEP	JENNY PENNY
TIN LIZZIE	ANGEL FACE
LORD SNOOTY	CHARLIE CHUTNEY
SMASHER	MINNIE THE MINX
CHARLIE THE CHIMP	RED RORY
KORKY THE CAT	PLUM MACDUFF
DENNIS THE MENACE	KAT and KANARY
BIFFO THE BEAR	PRINCE WHOOPEE
THE IRON FISH	THE HORSE THAT JACK BUILT
DESPERATE DAN	SHIPWRECK CIRCU.
LITTLE PLUM	BIRD BOY
PANSY POTTER	COCKY SUE
'FIGHTING FORKBEARD	WEE DAVIE and KING WILLIE
HUNGRY HORACE	

In the Fifties, long before mountain bikes, skateboards and roller blades, children took great pleasure in building 'soap-box' carts — four wheels, a plank, a wooden box and a bit of rope — to push (or pull) around.

Ginger's Super Jeep appeared on the pages of Dandy firstly as a text story, in 1955, then as a picture-strip in 1958 (from where these scenes were taken). Ginger's cart could do amazing things that no ordinary cart could do, and only Dandy readers could read all about them!

Over the page you'll see another 'cart-load' of funny stories!

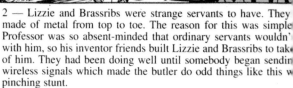

"STOP, thief! Bring back those wheels!" An angry yell echoed along the quiet street and brought Tin Lizzie, Professor Puffin's maid, rushing to an upstairs window to see what was wrong. *Bong!* No sooner had she thrown up the window than a pot bounced off her head. Lizzie was furious — but not about the pot hitting her. She was mad because Brassribs, the Professor's butler, had stolen the wheels off a pram belonging to a tramp.

2 — Lizzie and Brassribs were strange servants to have. They made of metal from top to toe. The reason for this was simple Professor was so absent-minded that ordinary servants wouldn' with him, so his inventor friends built Lizzie and Brassribs to tak of him. They had been doing well until somebody began sendin wireless signals which made the butler do odd things like this w pinching stunt.

3 — "He's off again!" Lizzie gasped, rushing down the stairs at top speed. That was a big mistake. The crafty Brassribs had expected this and it was one reason why he had taken up the floorboards at the bottom. Lizzie couldn't check her mad rush and into the cellar below she tumbled. Immediately Brassribs nailed planks over the hole.

4 — He saved one big plank, and hurried off with it, leaving Lizzie to roar and shout threats. Those queer wireless signals had made him act like a schoolboy once more. He took a drawer from a chest, and used the plank and the stolen wheels to turn it into a soap-box cart! Then off he went to see if he could find boys with whom he could play.

5 — Brassribs stopped some boys who we their way to school. "Who's going to school today?" he asked. They shook heads. Across the road was the school, a headmaster himself was standing by the "Old Beaky would give us a whacking caught us playing truant," one of the explained. "We daren't come."

6 — "So Beaky won't let you out?" the boyish butler rumbled. "Well, I'll fix him." In five minutes Brassribs was ready to "fix" the Headmaster. Unaware of the butler creeping up behind him with a large sack at the ready, the teacher stood scowling at the boys entering the school gates.

7 — "Hurry up, Johnston," he snapped at a boy sauntering past. Those were the last words he spoke to any of his boys for a long time. Brassribs whipped the sack down over his head, stifling the poor man's shout of alarm. "Got you, you tyrant!" the butler rumbled happily.

8 — Working quickly, Brassribs tied the securely round the teacher and dumped h the soap-box cart. Ignoring Beaky's m yells and threats, he dragged the cart away the school. And out from the gates sped daring lads, anxious to have a day off.

Meanwhile, in the locked cellar, Lizzie had ...d herself almost hoarse. But the Professor ...aving forty winks upstairs and hadn't ...her. Suddenly, to her surprise, the boards ...rised up above her head by the butler. ...le's going to let me out," she thought.

10 — But Brassribs had no intention of letting Lizzie out of her prison. Lizzie was just beginning to grin, thinking she would soon be free, when Brassribs vanished from the hole. A moment later he reappeared and heaved Beaky down on top of her. Lizzie crashed to the floor.

11 — Brassribs nailed the planks back into position. Then he left — not realising that he had presented Lizzie with a chance of escape. Lizzie pushed the teacher against the wall and climbed on to his shoulders. *Crash!* A blow from her fist shattered one of the boards.

Wasting no time, Lizzie enlarged the hole, climbed out, and ... the Headmaster up. Together they went looking for Brassribs. ...d by a rumbly voice booming out joyfully, they found the butler ...eep hill organising a race for soap-box carts. "Ready, steady — ...he bellowed. Downhill sped the carts. Then when the butler was ...ay down the hill, Lizzie and the teacher put a "Danger" sign ... his path.

13 — "Take that out of the way!" Brassribs bellowed. "Not likely," Lizzie piped. "You'd better stop." But Brassribs couldn't stop. Then a crafty grin spread over his face. He noticed a gap between the sign and the far side of the road, and like lightning he swerved his cart through this gap. Suddenly his grin faded. Right ahead was a nasty bend, far too sharp for him to turn. On the corner there was a sign which read, "DEAD SLOW. QUARRY."

...*Crash! Bang! Clatter! Crash!* Brassribs didn't manage to turn the ...r! "Ah, well," sighed Lizzie. "I suppose I'd better go and see if ...hurt." So, while the teacher rounded up the truants, Lizzie ...bled down the steep side of the quarry. What a tangled heap poor ...ribs was in! Bits of him were lying here, there and everywhere. ... dear me!" the metal maid moaned as she dumped the butler's ...ins into his cart. "What will the Professor say when he sees this ...of scrap?"

15 — When Lizzie reached the house, however, the Professor didn't say a thing. He was speechless! "I-I'll never be able to put all these bit together," he gasped when he found his voice. "What can I do, Lizzie?" "Never mind, Professor," the metal maid piped. "I'll do old Brassbrain's work until you have him repaired. And, anyway, when he's just a heap of scrap those wireless signals can't make him go haywire, can they?" Professor Puffin cheered up. Perhaps this was the end of their troubles for the time being.

ERIC and Dick Towers were staying at the Marsden Boarding House. They were amusing themselves doing a jig-saw puzzle—a big one that had a thousand and one pieces to it. But now it was nearly finished. They were glad, for it had taken the pair of them nearly all day.

2—But it took Charlie the Chimp only one second to undo their day's work! A piece of jig-saw had fallen under the table. Charlie, who had been watching keenly, spotted the missing piece and joyfully dived underneath the table to retrieve it. He was glad to be of some assistance to the lads.

3—Grinning all over his face, Cha came out from under the table. Bu straightened up too soon. His back ca the edge of the table and upset it, and moment the jig-saw was back into thousand and one pieces! "You clu fool!" roared Eric and Dick angrily.

4—Charlie slunk off, leaving the furious lads to pick up the pieces of their jig-saw. A run in his cart would cheer him up. Charlie fetched it out of the shed. But hello! Somebody had pinched a piece from it. Where was it? Charlie glanced around. *Ah, ha!* There it was, underneath that ladder.

5—With his eyes fixed firmly on his piece of wood, Charlie marched over and grabbed at it. *Heave! Heave! Heave!* Golly, it was hard to move! Charlie took an even firmer grip, took a deep, deep breath and heaved. Got it! All at once the piece of wood came free. Charlie went flying backwards.

6—*"Yooow!"* came a blood-curdling Charlie glanced up in complete aston ment. He was just in time to see his ma young Jack Marsden, taking a flying ba ward dive off a plank! Now why wa doing a silly thing like that? He might himself! Jack landed with a dull th

7—*SPLASH!* And a pot of paint he had been holding hit him! Jack was as red with rage as he was with paint! "You stupid, dundering idiot!" Jack thundered. "That piece of wood was there to keep my ladder steady!" Charlie realised now what an awful thing he had done. He had brought his master tumbling down from that scaffolding! But then, Jack shouldn't really have used his pet's piece of wood! Charlie took to his heels in a great hurry.

8—Jack was left to clean up and put his scaffolding toge again. Clumsy Charlie! That was the second time today he upset the apple cart. First the jig-saw, then the scaffolding. was having a gala day. And he wasn't finished yet! As he caree helter-skelter down the road, trouble loomed up dead ahea man was trundling a barrow-load of stone slabs into his gar Charlie quickly let out a chimpy yell of warning.

As if Smasher didn't wreck enough in his cart, the Dandy had another fun-pal who was a cart-load of trouble — Charlie the Chimp! Although a chimpanzee, Charlie acted as porter in a small boarding house, usually causing mayhem as he tried to 'help' people!

9.9.59

—But the warning died in his throat. *CRASH!* Charlie's cart ...ked straight into the side of the barrow. The impact sent ...lie whizzing forward, over the top. The barrow tilted—and out ...e heavy stone slabs on to the ground. *CRASH!* Mr Wilkie had ...he shaft of his barrow being wrenched out of his hands. He ...d round in plenty of time to see his slabs become dozens of ...hed pieces. Oh dear! Another upset apple cart!

10—Charlie picked himself up off the ground and fled. "You blind dolt!" yelled Mr Wilkie. "You've smashed all my paving stones!" And to emphasise his point Mr Wilkie threw a piece of the smashed stones at Charlie. It missed narrowly. But Charlie was worried about his cart. It, too, was in pieces! Perhaps he could go back and collect the pieces later. So Charlie waited. Then he crept back when the coast was clear. His smashed cart was still there.

—And so was the piece of stone Mr ...kie had thrown at him. Charlie picked ...he stone and peeped over the hedge to ...what Mr Wilkie was doing. The poor ... was piecing the smashed stones into ...azy paving. Charlie chuckled and ...kily held aloft the piece of stone he had.

12—Mr Wilkie shook his fist angrily. "Be off, you cheeky wretch!" he roared. Charlie dropped the stone over the hedge. Mr Wilkie would need it for his jig-saw! Then he went off home, chuckling. The lounge window was open. Charlie decided to take a short cut in on the curtains.

13—*CRASH!* A large vase had been sitting on a sideboard by the window as Charlie came swinging in. Now the vase was on the floor in at least a hundred pieces! Charlie was aghast. Upsetting Jack on the scaffolding was bad enough, but smashing his precious vase was worse!

—But Charlie is a clever and cunning ...ap. If he glued the pieces of vase ...ther Jack would never know that it had ...n smashed—or so Charlie hoped. ...rlie got on with it. He was almost ...hed when Eric and Dick spotted him.

15—Revenge shone in their eyes. Under Charlie's table was a piece of the vase. Eric dived for it—and in rising upset the table exactly as Charlie had done earlier. The vase crashed to the ground. "Oh, have we smashed your vase, Charlie?" giggled Eric.

16—"No, you've smashed *my* vase!" boomed Jack, coming in at that moment. The boys stammered their protests. Jack wouldn't heed them. "You'll pay!" he ordered. Charlie hid the glue. Everything might come unstuck if Jack spotted that!

Ever wondered what Dennis the Menace does all day? Well, this secret document was found folded up inside an old homework jotter that had been "lost" somewhere between school and Dennis's house! Have a look at Dennis's busy day, then turn the page for a special section featuring the exploits of Dennis the Menace through the Fifties!

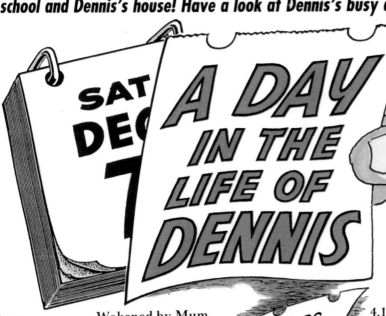

A DAY IN THE LIFE OF DENNIS

8 a.m.	—Wakened by Mum.
8.1 a.m.	—Fast asleep.
8.15 a.m.	—Wakened by Dad.
8.16 a.m.	—Fast asleep.
8.30 a.m.	—Wakened by slipper.
8.35 a.m.	—Go to bathroom for thorough wash.
8.36 a.m.	—Leave bathroom.
8.40 a.m.	—Eat my breakfast.
8.45 a.m.	—Eat Dad's breakfast.
8.50 a.m.	—Set out for school.
10.30 a.m.	—Arrive at school.
10.31 a.m.	—Punished.
10.35 a.m.	—Start doing lessons.
10.36 a.m.	—Stop doing lessons and start firing inky pellets at Teacher.
12.30 p.m.	—Get out of school.
12.35 p.m.	—Eat my dinner.
12.40 p.m.	—Eat Dad's dinner.
12.42 p.m.	—Kicked out of house to make sure I reach school on time.

2.45 p.m.	—Don't reach school on time.
2.46 p.m.	—Punished.
2.50-3.50 p.m.	—Have a short nap.
3.51 p.m.	—Pick a fight with Walter.
3.52 p.m.	—Fight over. Am put out of room. (Suits me! It was all a crafty plan to get out of school early!)

4.15 p.m.	—Eat my tea.
4.16 p.m.	—Don't eat Dad's tea. (He's working late tonight so that I can't!)
4.30 p.m.	—Mum insists I stay in and do my homework.
4.31 p.m.	—Finish homework. Go out to play with Curly.
4.32-8.55 p.m.	—Play with Curly. Fight with everybody else.
9 p.m.	—Eat supper.
9.5 p.m.	—Eat Dad's tea and supper combined when he's not looking.
9.10 p.m.	—Dad looks.
9.11-9.15 p.m.	—Receive severe spanking.
9.16 p.m.	—Sent to bed in disgrace. Light turned off.
9.17-10 p.m.	—Read "BEANO" under bedclothes by torchlight.
10.1 p.m.	—Dad hears me laughing. Comes in and snaffles "BEANO". (Bet he wants to read it himself!)
10.5-10.30 p.m.	—Lie thinking up mischief for tomorrow.
10.30 p.m.-8 a.m.	—ZZZZZZZZZZZZ!

NURSERY

Ever wonder what Dennis the Men[ac]e was like as a baby? Well, wonder [no] more! This hilarious tale is from a [...] Dennis The Menace Book.

DENNIS hasn't always been a bad boy. Go on — [...] you don't believe it. But it's true. Before Dennis [was] a bad boy, he was a horrible baby, see? Now you be[lieve] me, don't you?

You know how on Father's Day, most dads get l[ovely] surprise presents. Well, one terrible year on Father's D[ay I] got Dennis instead. That's when he was born. I'll n[ever] forget that day, no matter how hard I try, so you'll fo[rgive] me if I don't say anything about it.

The next important event in Dennis's life was the[day] his first tooth appeared. I was the unlucky chap [who] discovered it — and I've got the scar on my right th[umb] to prove it. What a gnasher it was! When he was hu[ngry] Dennis used to gnaw chunks out of his cot with that to[oth.] It was soon reinforced by nineteen other fangs and [you] will not be surprised when I tell you that one morn[ing I] went into Dennis's room and found that the cot [had] disappeared. The bold boy was lying happily amo[ng a] heap of wood shavings.

When Dennis was one year old we threw a party. [...]

CRIMES

OR
DENNIS GROWING UP

I'll always remember the day. He had been snapping and snarling for months when suddenly his lips began to twitch suspiciously.

"Mum!" I yelled to his mother in the kitchen. "I think he's going to speak. Fetch the neighbours — quick!"

And so a large crowd of grown-ups soon gathered round Dennis's pram waiting with bated breath.

"Bet he says 'Dada'," I chuckled, my chest swelling with pride.

"No!" said Mum decisively. "I'm sure it's going to be 'Mama'. Look at the way his mouth's working."

"Quiet now," I whispered. "Here it comes."

In complete silence Dennis looked round at the admiring group clustered about him. Then his big eyes settled on me, and I smirked. The little darling was going to prove Mum wrong. But we were both wrong.

Still staring up at me Dennis spoke his first word —

"FISHFACE!"

"HAW! HAW! HAW!" The neighbours rolled on the floor with mirth.

"I'm glad you're enjoying yourselves!" I hooted. "Don't slam the door as you go out!"

ord "threw" intentionally, because that's what Dennis
ith the cake. I'm still trying to get the stains off my
suit. He ate the candle, of course. You'll pardon me if
nothing about the lad's other parties. I wouldn't like
nt in the middle of writing this story.

ortly after that historic party, a Flower Show was
in our town. It was Mum's idea to enter Dennis in the
Beautiful Baby Contest, always a popular event at
how. I was against it, of course. But there was a slight
ce that the other entrants might be baby gorillas, so
Dennis was duly entered.

u may be astonished to know that he won a prize. But
will not be surprised when I tell you that it was for
the UGLIEST baby at the show. He would have won
prize even if the other competitors HAD been baby
las.

s my face red! It certainly was, because just at that
ent Dennis, in his lovable way, started throwing prize
toes at me.

was a long time before Dennis spoke his first word.

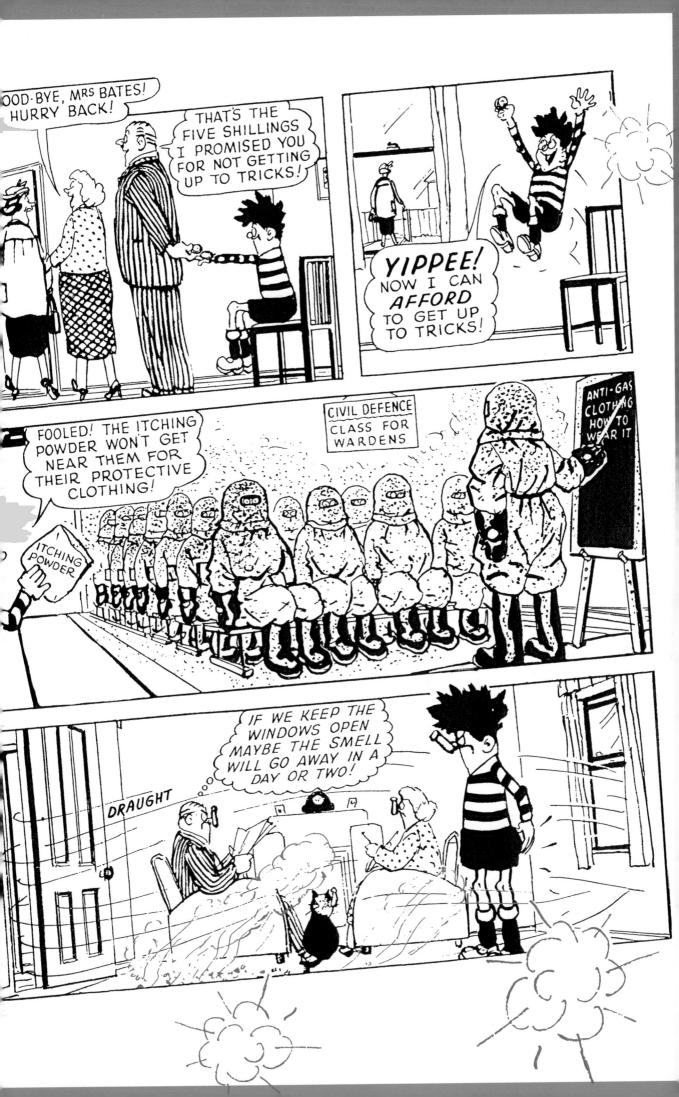

DOCTOR'S ORDERS

DAD IN DISGRACE

DENNIS the MENACE

12.5.59

IF YOU WANT TO KEEP WARM, GO FOR A WALK — AND DO YOUR "DAILY DOZEN" WHILE YOU'RE ABOUT IT!

SHIVER

ARMS SIDEWAYS—

—STRETCH!

ZONK!

THE "SNOW-DROPS" ARE EARLY THIS YEAR!

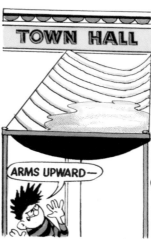

TOWN HALL

ARMS UPWARD—

SPLOSH!

—STRETCH!

OUTSIDE THE RITZY HOTEL, A LITTLE LAD IS PUTTING THE FINISHING TOUCHES TO HIS SNOWMAN, WHEN—

THE RITZY HO

ARMS SIDEWAYS— STRETCH!

ARMS FORWARD— STRETCH!

WOOSH!

SNORE!

DING!

DING!

I'VE BEEN TRAILING YOU, YOU MENACE! TRUST YOU TO MAKE IT HOT FOR OTHER PEOPLE, TOO, WHILE YOU WARMED YOURSELF UP!

THE RIT

HOME SWEET HOME.

FORWARD BEND — WHILE I DO MY DAILY DOZEN!

Teddy the Bear . . . Biffo Teddy . . . er . . . Biffo the Bear is dressed in typical Fifties-style young people's clothing . . . padded jacket, drainpipe trousers, and a bow fly . . . butter-tie . . . er . . . butterfly, in this 1957 tie-tale!

THE IRON FISH

1—THE Iron Fish sparkled and shone in the bright sunlight which streamed through the open doorway of a boatshed on the busy sea-front of Rio de Janeiro, in South America. Young Danny Gray, better known as Deep-Sea Danny, the owner of this wonderful mechanical fish, watched closely as a squad of expert mechanics worked hard, putting the finishing touches to a complete overhaul which the boy had ordered for his strange craft. The mechanics were all crew members of the Tarpon, a yacht owned by Professor Gray, Danny's father and inventor of the amazing Iron Fish. At present, the Tarpon was lying at anchor in the bay. Bill Knight, the Tarpon's chief engineer, clapped his hand to Danny's shoulder and pointed to the craft. "It'll be ready in half an hour!" he promised. "Then you can take it out and put it through its paces! I can promise you it'll be in first-rate condition."

6—Fortunately, Danny and the two men were good swimmers. While his friends struck out for the upturned boat, Danny's first thought was for the safety of his Iron Fish. He was relieved to find it still afloat, half-submerged in the water. Then, angrily wondering who had been at the helm of the motor launch that was responsible for his unexpected ducking, the lad waited anxiously while the operation of lifting the Iron Fish was carried out. Under his watchful eyes, the Fish was at last lowered safely on to the deck. Because the cockpit had been open when the Fish was swamped, the craft was half-full of water and a check on the fittings would have to be made.

7—Danny waited, clinging to the upturned boat, as which had been thrown from the launch drifted towards floated by, the lad reached out his hand and lifted the wh out of the water. The article was nothing more than a han Disappointed, for Danny had hoped it might provide so to the owner of the dangerously-handled launch, the b the handkerchief into his shirt pocket. Meanwhile, Bill K hailed the Tarpon and already the yacht was on the mo

2—Half an hour later, the Iron Fish was launched and, with Danny settled in the cockpit, was towed out to the open water by a small motor boat from the Tarpon. Then, with a cheery wave to Bill Knight, Danny closed the cockpit cover and pressed the starter button on the dashboard in front of him. At once, the powerful electric motor inside the Fish whirred into life.

3—Eyes alight with keen anticipation of what was in store—for there was nothing he liked better than to be at the controls of his Iron Fish—Danny put the long, silvery craft into a dive. Next, he zoomed for the surface and, with a thrust of its tail, the Fish broke the calm sea and soared high into the air before re-entering the water.

8—When the Tarpon reached the friends in the water, a rope-ladder was quickly dropped over the side of the yacht. Thankfully, Danny and the two men clambered aboard. But before removing his wet clothes, the lad waited anxiously while the operation of lifting the Iron Fish was carried out.

9—As soon as Bill Knight had changed into dry clo started on a close inspection of the Fish. Confident wonderful craft was in good hands, Danny went off to his ease, when an urgent voice interrupted the musi listening to on a radio. "It is reported that Laura King been kidnapped!" crackled the announcer's voice. "She is daughter of Henry Kingsman, millionaire oil magnate.

4—As he made the Fish dive, leap and swim, better than any swordfish, Danny grinned with delight. The Iron Fish was performing perfectly. The mechanics had done a good job. Alongside the Tarpon's boat, young Danny congratulated Bill Knight. "It couldn't be better," enthused the boy. As the boy talked about the test, the deep roar of a powerful motor engine was heard.

5—Danny turned to see a rakish-looking m approaching at high speed. With only inches to s the Fish. Next second, the high wash, left moving launch, swamped the Iron F boat. Danny and his friends w speedboat raced past, he

e had been lowered over th Back in the Iron Fish, youn he plane off the water. As it ch ssed the starter button on the d fted steadily across the calm oc neiro was lost to sight over t ast waters.

Danny was j n a red light winked on the dashboard. "A radio muttered Danny. "I hope it's good news." He lifted headphones, set them on his head, and spoke into a mi itted to the dashboard. "Danny here!" he said. "Wh through the headphones crackled Bob Hartley's voice "I've sighted a whalers' factory ship!" he reported. " own to take a look." "Be careful—and good luck!" replied

his way quickly through the busy South America. The big city was kidnapping of Laura Kingsman, ng in the Brazilian capital. Special s were on sale carrying news of th ieged at every street corner. But paper. He knew more than the e kidnapping and he was on his way t portant information.

2—Less than an hour ago, Danny had been giving his wond Iron Fish a trial run when a powerful launch had passed the "Laura" embroidered across one corner. That was enoug Danny! Now, in the police headquarters, he showed a sergeant handkerchief and told his story. At once, the sergeant beckon orderly while Danny studied a picture of the kidnapped gir police poster.

3—The South American police sergeant was quick to understand the importance of Danny's information. "Take this boy to the Chief!" he ordered and, a few minutes later, the orderly was ushering Danny into the office of the city's Chief of Police. Quickly, Danny repeated his story and produced the tell-tale handkerchief. At once the Chief lifted the telephone on his desk. "Contact the Air Force Base!" he rapped out. "This is an emergency!"

4—The Police Chief was quickly in touch with the officer at the Air Force Base. He told Danny's story an search to be made from the air for the mysterious launch. No tim was wasted at the airfield. Five minutes after the telephone call w made, four jet aircraft left the ground to search the seas for the kidnappers while, back at police headquarters, Danny waited impatiently for the pilots' reports.

m the Fish, Bob Ha nce. "Be careful" th hing to worry about here. An below. Bob shrugged his shoulders. ed and banked his plane.

eaplane dived steeply towards the stern of the F was surprised to see members of the crew scuttling ne deck. They seemed to be afraid of the plane. hardened. There was something suspicious about the Expertly, Bob levelled his plane as he flew alongside the Suddenly, from the bridge, there came a burst of machine-gu

5—But, five hours later, there was still no report of the launch being sighted and the aircraft returned to refuel. "That launch seems to have vanished into thin air!" exclaimed the Police Chief. Danny left police headquarters and, in his Iron Fish, returned to his father's yacht, the Tarpon. The boy's face was grim.

6—On board the yacht, Danny quickly sought out Bob Hartley, the young pilot of the seaplane which the Tarpon carried on deck. "I've a hunch that launch has been taken aboard a larger vessel," explained Danny. "Maybe you could find it!" Bob nodded. "I'll do anything to catch the rats," he said grimly.

11—Meanwhile, far away, Danny was waiting for Bob to report, his eyes glued to the bulb on the dashboard. When it glowed red, the boy started forward expectantly. Suddenly, he heard the pilot's alarmed voice come through the headphones. "They're firing at me!" he yelled. "The plane's hit! She's out of control." Bob's voice was abruptly silenced by the sound of a rending crash, and Danny's heart almost skipped a beat.

12—Madly, the boy tore off his headphones and stabbed at the starter button of his Fish. The motor whined as the boy sent the long, gleaming craft surging through the water at full speed. Danny bit his lip. Bob's voice had revealed only too clearly what had happened. Somewhere, miles ahead, the seaplane had been shot down. It seemed that Bob had found a vital clue in the search for Laura Kingsman and lost his life in so doing.

HARTLEY clung desperately to the fuselage of his sea-half-submerged in the calm waters of the South Atlantic, miles from the sea-front of Rio de Janeiro, in South America. Less than half an hour before, Bob's plane had been badly shot down by machine-gun fire from the bridge of a factory ship—the vessel which Bob had suspected might hold the kidnappers of Laura Kingsman, the daughter of a sea captain. Just before he was shot down, Bob managed to radio his young friend, Danny Gray, owner of the Iron Fish. Now, Bob waited for Danny to come to his aid. At last, he spotted the gleaming Fish surging through the waves towards him, with Danny at the controls.

2— Danny helped the pilot into the roomy cockpit of the Fish and listened, grim-faced, as Bob told what had happened. "As soon as they shot me down, they steamed on," concluded the pilot. "I reckon the crew were mighty scared I'd find out something they wanted to hide." "Laura Kingsman!" said Danny grimly, and sent the Fish surging full speed through the water in pursuit of the kidnappers' factory ship. It was Danny who had first picked up the kidnappers' trail when he recovered a handkerchief thrown from a speeding launch in Rio de Janeiro's harbour. Embroidered on the handkerchief was the name "Laura." Danny reported his find to the police and a search was made for the mysterious launch. But the boat had completely disappeared.

"My hunch is that the launch is hidden aboard that factory ship," said Danny. "If it is, Laura Kingsman will be aboard, too!" added agreement. "I can't think of any other reason for shooting me down in cold blood!" he said. At high speed, the Fish through the water, but it was dusk by the time the friends reached the stern. Silently, the Fish crept up to the stern.

4— There was a wide opening at the stern of the ship, which was specially designed to deal with the whales caught by the smaller whale-catching ships. A ramp led to the upper deck. This was the ramp up which the dead whales were hauled. Soon the Iron Fish reached the ramp and the two friends stepped out. As quietly as possible they pulled the Fish out of the water.

7— The pair reached a long, dimly-lit corridor without incident. "I wonder where the girl is being kept," breathed Danny into the pilot's ear. Suddenly, Bob gripped the boy's arm as the sound of footsteps came from the end of the corridor. Desperately, the pair searched about them for somewhere to hide. Luckily, some barrels and coils of rope were piled up against a bulkhead and the friends crouched down behind these. And only just in time! Down the corridor came stalking a tall, swarthy-faced man dressed in a dark lounge suit. He held a bunch of keys.

8— This city type was followed by another man, wearing an apron and carrying a mug and a plate of food. Danny and Bob held their breath as the pair stopped and the first man unlocked a nearby cabin door. Danny risked a peep over the top of the barrel. His eyes widened. Through the open cabin doorway he could see a small, dark-haired girl. Laura Kingsman! So interested were Bob and Danny in what they saw, they did not hear soft footsteps on the companionway behind their backs. Then a blaze of torchlight lit up their hiding place! One of the crew had stumbled upon them.

9—As Bob and Danny started to their feet in surprise, the seaman let out a yell. "Get him, Bob!" shouted Danny, and he threw himself forward to grab the man about the knees. As the seaman buckled, Bob's fist smashed against his chin. With a groan, the seaman dropped to the deck, unconscious.

10— Next second, the friends were haring up the companionway to the upper deck. But, though they had acted swiftly, the seaman's yell had roused the silent ship. As Bob and Danny raced across the deck to the ramp, bullets began to whistle about their heads and the beam of a searchlight lit up their running figures.

11— But, miraculously, Bob and Danny came unharmed through the hail of bullets and, panting for breath, they reached the shelter of the ramp. "We'll make it!" gasped Danny. "Get the Fish into the water!" leapt into the cockpit while Bob strained to push the ramp. From the top of the ramp friends.

12—Silently, the Iron Fish slid into the water and Bob leapt into the cockpit beside Danny. The boy pressed a button on the dashboard. Whirr! As the motor started up, he closed the cockpit cover. Then Danny put his wonderful craft into a dive. Swiftly, the Fish began to submerge, only yards from the ship, while a searchlight from the bridge swept over the water towards them.

the other man, had the rescue to the hour at for speed.

kidnappers are on the "at they're up face, Danny saw Laura, killed aboard in the arms of ance away. At ome the factory HALF way.

fast launch soon reached the island and moved through a narrow lagoon. At a touch of a button the Iron Fish on the water and at the height of its leap Danny was able launch heading for a sandy beach.

2—From the air Bob Hartley spotted the factory ship and wirelessed to Danny in the Iron Fish that he was going down to have a closer look. As the plane neared the ship it had been brought down by a burst of machine-gun fire. The vessel had steamed on, leaving Bob to his fate. In the nick of time, Danny had appeared in the Iron Fish to rescue Bob. The speedy Fish soon caught up with the factory ship and after dark Danny and Bob boarded the ship to find the launch they were looking for stored on deck and hidden beneath a tarpaulin. They had also seen Laura Kingsman before they were discovered and forced to make their getaway. Now, for hours, Danny and Bob had secretly followed the factory ship, waiting for something to happen. At last the ship stopped.

"I don't remember seeing that island on our charts," said Danny. "You'd better contact the yacht, Bob." The pilot switched on the Fish's radio and spoke into the microphone. "Iron Fish calling Tarpon. Laura Kingsman being taken to uncharted island figures three five zero miles south-east of Rio. Over." At the wireless operator aboard the Tarpon acknowledged Bob's message, Danny sent the Iron Fish speeding after the launch. "We'll keep the thugs under observation until help arrives," said Danny grimly.

6—Purposefully, Danny stopped the Fish some distance off shore. Night was falling. "I'm going ashore to scout that island," he told Bob. "The more we know about the place the more information we can give the rescue party when they arrive!"

7— The lad dived cleanly into the water and struck out strongly for the shore. As Danny swam off he heard Bob calling after him. "Don't do anything rash, kid. That launch ashore don't pull any punches. Pull out fast if there's any sign of trouble." With strong strokes, Danny headed for the reef. Over. Then, swimming for long distances under water, he reached the launch beached across the lagoon. Footprints in the sand showed clearly the path which the kidnappers had taken.

8—In the steamy tropical atmosphere, Danny followed the trail of trampled vegetation which the crooks had left when smashing their way through the undergrowth. Then, suddenly, the lad almost blundered into a clearing in which stood a fair-sized bungalow, raised on piles. Lights blazed in the place and, for a moment, Danny saw Laura Kingsman's shadow against a blind. It was obvious that the girl was being badly treated. The boy's hands clenched in bitter anger. "The fiends!" he said under his breath.

9— Danny kept watch on the house until he was confident that the kidnappers intended to settle in. Then he set out to explore the island before dark, prowling around and noting the layout of the place. At last, satisfied, the boy made his way back to the shore and dimly made out the shape of the Fish lying in the water. With his waterproof torch Danny guided Bob by its beam until the pilot brought the Iron Fish slowly into shore. The big Fish grounded gently on the mud. "Everything all right, Danny?" whispered Bob from the cockpit. Quickly, Danny outlined the situation.

10— Now came the task of getting the Fish on to the land and under cover. The chums couldn't risk leaving it on the open shore. "It's gonna be a tough job, Danny!" muttered Bob, eyeing the marshy land over which they would have to drag the Fish. Straining every muscle, the two friends moved the Fish inch by inch over the soggy earth. At times, when the craft settled in a particularly marshy spot, it seemed as if it was stuck for good, but by superhuman efforts Bob and Danny at last had the big Fish at what they thought was a safe distance from the shore.

Limp with exhaustion, the pals had a breather before starting to collect foliage with which to camouflage their craft. There was no difficulty in finding suitable plants for this job. "We'll soon be finished now, Bob," whispered Danny. "Then we can look for a place to hole up for the night." As Danny finished speaking, a rustling sound came from the foliage above them.

12— "What was that?" hissed Bob. Both he and Danny stood tensely listening, but nothing could be seen or heard except the busy hum of mosquitoes. "Probably a bird," said Danny in a low voice as the tension eased. Then, suddenly, the lad heard a thud and scream of terror from Bob. Turning, he saw the pilot in the coils of a huge boa-constrictor, the deadliest crushing snake in the world.

IN semi-darkness Danny Gray, young owner of the Iron Fish, pointed a Very pistol at the swaying head of a great boa-constrictor that had caught his pal, Bob Hartley, in its crushing coils. The snake had dropped swiftly to hide the Iron Fish beneath a nearby tree as the pair were working to hide the Iron Fish from a covering of leaves and palm branches. Danny steadied his shaking hand and fired the pistol point-blank at the reptile's head. A great flash lit the darkness and then Bob Hartley felt the snake slide to the ground, where it lay quite still. With a shudder of relief Bob Hartley staggered clear, to lean exhausted against the tree.

2—Hurriedly, Danny began again to cover the long, gleaming Iron Fish with tropical foliage. The life of a little girl was at stake. Danny and Bob Hartley, seaplane pilot on Danny's father's yacht, had come to rescue Laura Kingsman, the daughter of a millionaire, from her kidnappers. Danny and Bob had followed them in the Iron Fish to a lonely island off the coast of South America, and radioed for help before beaching the Fish and hiding it on the island. Now the desperate measure which Danny had taken to save Bob's life had alerted the kidnappers. As the slow-burning flare lit up the sky for several seconds, its glow was visible for miles around.

3—On the veranda of the house which the kidnappers were using as a hideout, one of the gang spotted the light and called anxiously to his friend. "See that, Jake? There's something queer going on out there!" Jake's hard eyes narrowed to slits. "You'd better take a look-see, Dingo. Take your gun an' if anything moves give it the works!" he said viciously. With his revolver at the ready, Dingo cautiously made his way to where the light had come from, stopping every few moments to sweep the shadows with the powerful torch which he was carrying.

4—Meanwhile, Dan... camouflage the Fish. Then th... cockpit. "That flare's bound to attract the s... Bob, and hope that they miss us," whispered Danny tensely. At last they heard Dingo's footsteps draw nearer. They heard th... kidnapper stop and prod the body of the boa-constrictor. Then h... filled the cockpit as Dingo swung his torch over the foliage... covered it. Danny had a sinking feeling that they h... discovered. He stabbed at a button on the Fish's con...

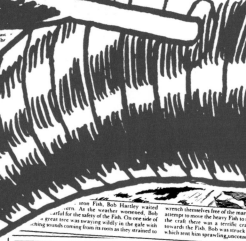

5—Immediately the tail of the Fish lashed round, catching Dingo a stunning blow which sent the crook flying backwards. Before the kidnapper could rise to his feet, Danny leaped from the cockpit and pinned the dazed crook to the ground.

6—In a few minut... from the Fish's tor... Dingo had dropp... that we have a...

7—Earlier, Danny had made himself familiar with the layout of the island and this stood him in good stead now. He had no difficulty in locating the kidnappers' house even in the darkness. Lightly, as a cat, the lad made his way on to the veranda. With a thrust of his hand he pushed open the door and burst into the room. Jake didn't even have time to turn before Danny barked, "Hands up and no monkey business!" The crook hesitated for a moment then slowly raised his hands above his head. Laura Kingsman was in the room, tied to a chair.

8—Satisfied that Jake was not going to give any troubl... motioned to Laura. "Untie the girl and make it quick," D... the pistol trained steadily on him. He was taki... character as slippery as Jake... noticed the open do... boy. As La... "You—"

HEAD... tropic... way along t... magnate, had... thin South Amer... Fish, Danny and... Dingo, one of the ki... Laura and left the othe... cupboard in the bungalow...

...n had broken as Danny and Laura were making... k to the spot where the Iron Fish was beached. Bob... e there guarding the Fish and the gangster. Dingo... ng, Laura!" yelled Danny above the howling wind... ararly there" As the storm eased, Danny and Laura made... progress, but, when they reached their rendezvous, Danny... up in horror at the sight before him. The Fish was pinned... fter a great tree which lay sprawled, unconscious. He had been... eside it Bob Hartley lay sprawled, unconscious. He had been... struck down by the tree.

...Iron Fish, Bob Hartley waited... orm. As the weather worsened, Bob... arful for the safety of the Fish. On one side of... great tree was swaying wildly in the gale with... ching sounds coming from its roots as they strained to...

...wrench themselves free of the marshy ground. The pilot decided... attempt to move the heavy Fish to safety. As Bob put his shoulder... the craft there was a terrific crack and the great tree crash... towards the Fish. Bob was struck on the head by a thick bran... which sent him sprawling, unconscious to the ground.

7—Jake chuckled contemptuously as he stepped over the prostrate boy and picked up the fallen revolver. "Fancy dat stupid kid thinking he could put one over me an' get away with it. Now to find out what's happened to dat fool, Dingo, and get the millionaire's kid back in my hands again." Stealthily, Jake Morelli made his way to where the Iron Fish lay pinned beneath the fallen tree. With his pistol levelled at Bob, he burst through the foliage. "Put your mitts up, wise guy," he snarled.

8—The ruthless glint in the crook's eyes warned Bob tha... no option. Expertly, Jake drew a knife and slashed toward... pinning Dingo's arms. Then the crook moved cautiously f... and snatched Laura away from Bob's side. "She's da one we... he snarled. "You back up against da nearest palm tree, bec... Swiftly, the crooks lashed the pilot to the tree. "We mig... back an' pay ya a flying visit when we've got da ransom... sneered Jake, as the crooks led Laura off.

3—Anxiously, Danny rushed forward and felt his friend's... With a sigh of relief he found it still beating strongly. With an ch... Danny and Laura raised the bulky pilot to a sitting position, and... few minutes later Bob slowly regained consciousness. "How are you, Bob?" asked Danny, anxiously. The pilot rubbed his head ruefully. "I feel a bit groggy, kid. The tree hit me before I could dodge it, but it takes more than that to put paid to old Hartley!"

9—Meanwhile, Danny recovered slowly from Jake's knock-out... ow and dragged himself upright with the help of a veranda... pport. Then, on the distant beach, he saw a sight which brought... m swiftly back to his senses—Laura was being dragged towards... launch which had brought the kidnappers to the island. Danny... ained. He realised he could not reach the beach in time to do... thing to hinder the crooks leaving.

10—"A rifle! That's what I need," thought Dan... desperation, the lad began to rummage through the sh... inside the wrecked house, hoping to find a weapon he co... against the crooks. After a hectic search, the boy found... wanted—a heavy calibre rifle and several boxes of amm... lying under a partition which had been knocked flat du... storm.

5—The storm had passed as Danny made his way back to the kidnappers' hideout. Cautiously, Danny drew his pistol, which he had taken from Dingo. It was quite possible that the tough Jake Morelli had smashed his way out of his prison. The boy was taking no chances. When Danny emerged into the clearing where the bungalow stood, he saw that the storm had played havoc with the building.

6—Doors had been ripped away. Shutters and windows had been smashed, and the whole structure lay at a crazy angle with its roof caved in. Danny moved cautiously towards the ruin. Suddenly, he heard a noise behind him and turned swiftly—then everything went black. The crafty Jake Morelli had tossed a stone into the jungle to distract the lad's attention, then leaped from cover and struck Danny down.

...The lad snatched up the weapon and a handful of ammunition then raced out on to the veranda. Already, the launch was turning and moving away from the shore. Hurriedly, Danny loaded the bullets into the magazine and lined up the sights on the crooks' boat. The speeding, bobbing launch was no easy target. All the lad could hope for was that one of his shots would destroy a vital part of the launch's engine.

12—CRACK! CRACK! CRACK! Danny worked the rifl... at top speed in an effort to get in as many shots as possible... the launch moved out of range. Soon the magazine was emp... still the fast launch raced on. Sick at heart, Danny laid do... rifle. It looked as if the crooks were to get clean away. But... launch, Jake Morelli let out a yell as he spotted a strea... pouring from a bullet hole in the boat's side.

...sinking heart, Danny Gray, owner of the amazing Iron ...hed a motor launch speed out of the island lagoon and ...he open sea. On board the boat were Laura Kingsman, ...of a millionaire, and Jake Morelli and Dingo, two ...of the gang which had kidnapped her. The kidnapping ...place in Rio de Janeiro, South America, where Danny's ...cht, Tarpon, was anchored. In the Iron Fish, the lad and ...Tarpon's seaplane pilot, had trailed the ship which ...put ashore on a lonely island off ...ing for help, Bob and Danny ...er observation.

2—The friends had clashed with the kidnappers and rescued Laura, but only for a short time. In a tropical storm, a tree crashed on the Iron Fish and gave the gangsters time to recapture Laura and make their getaway. In a last effort Danny tried rifle fire hoping to cripple the launch. Unknown to the lad, one of his shots had punctured the boat's fuel tank, but when the launch proceeded on its way, Danny thought he had failed. The boy picked up an axe which was lying on the ground beside the bungalow and made his way back to the Fish which was still trapped beneath a fallen tree. There, he found Bob tied to a tree where the kidnappers had left him. Danny's axe made short work of the ropes which bound the Tarpon's pilot.

...unk splintered and broke. The Fish was free ...another job like that in a hurry," panted Bob ...fully, Danny checked every control on the ...ef when he found them all working to his ...a tough little craft.

7—Danny was right. The crooks had not gone very far. In fact, by leaving the island, Danny and Bob were moving away from the kidnappers and their prisoner. After Jake had spotted the fuel leak, he had ordered Dingo to circle and the crooks had beached their launch on the opposite side of the island. With an ugly scowl on his face, Jake inspected the damage and snarled viciously, "No use patching the hole up an' going on. There ain't enough fuel left to drive a scooter ten yards!"

8—"We're in a tight spot. What's the next move, Jake?" asked Dingo. "We've got a radio, ain't we, stupid?" snapped Jake at his slow-thinking accomplice. "Just because YOU don't know how to work it doesn't mean it ain't any good." Jake switched on the launch's small but powerful transmitter and netted into the frequency used by the ship which had brought them to the island. The gangster kept repeating the ship's call sign until he received an answer. "Get the Captain. I've a message for him," he said urgently.

9—When the rascally Captain heard Jake's account of what had happened on the island, his fist clenched in anger. "The bungling fools!" he spluttered. "They payed me a fat price to take 'em to that island, but I didn't figure on this. They need help. If they're caught, they'll squeal on me." Muttering angrily, the Captain moved out on to the wing of the bridge and gave the order for the ship's helicopter crew to get airborne.

10—Meanwhile, Danny was driving the Iron Fish to the limit in an attempt to overtake the kidnappers. Any moment they expected to catch sight of the crippled launch out at sea. So keen were the pals on scanning the ocean for the crippled boat that they failed to spot the helicopter until it was quite near. Suddenly, Danny pointed upwards and let out an excited shout. "I'll bet it's a Rio police 'copter! They got our wireless message!"

The pals yelled and cheered. With the helicopter to aid ...could cover a tremendous area of ocean and were sure ...unch. Danny stopped the Fish and the pals waved ...act the attention of the helicopter crew. However, ...helicopter were not feeling so friendly. One of ...sub machine-gun and cocked it as his ...the tiny craft below them.

12—"They must be the pair that've been givin' Jake and Dingo all the trouble," growled the man with the gun to the pilot. "Hover over them and I'll let them have it!" The thug slid back the helicopter's door and fired a long burst at the Fish. Bob and Danny were almost numbed by shock as the bullets slammed off the metal craft. The shooting was good and the next burst was certain to smash into the cockpit.

...sh chatter of machine-gun fire shattered the peaceful ...the South Atlantic as a murderous attack took place ...nny Gray's Iron Fish. Hovering above the Fish was a ...attack took place so suddenly that for a moment ...numbed and shocked in the cockpit. Then he snapped ...cockpit cover and put the Fish into a steep dive. Swiftly ...ly the Iron Fish slid below the surface while bullets ...water to foam above it. Safe below the surface, Danny ...Fish off.

2—In the cockpit beside Danny was Bob Hartley, pilot on Danny's father's yacht, Tarpon. While the ...anchored in the harbour at Rio de Janeiro, Laura Kingsman, millionaire's daughter, had been kidnapped. In the Iron Fish, Danny and Bob trailed the ship which had taken Laura and her kidnappers to a lonely island off the coast. Danny and Bob tried unsuccessfully to rescue Laura while the kidnappers, Dingo and Jake Morelli, radioed to their ship for help. The vessel's rascally captain had sent the helicopter to aid the crooks and Danny and Bob had mistaken the machine for a police craft from Rio.

...the Iron Fish glided through the water, a giant swordfish ...from the depths. The great fish swished its tail angrily as ...at it thought was a rival. Suddenly, it rushed forward and ...e Iron Fish a terrific blow. It was as if the Fish had been ...a gigantic hammer. Danny and Bob lurched to one side ...pit, startled by the unexpected attack.

4—Forced to the surface by the impact, the friends saw their monstrous attacker for the first time. The great swordfish surged to the attack again, but Danny was in no mood to fight it. He gave the Iron Fish full throttle and streaked for the island with the huge swordfish in hot pursuit. "We'll be safe once we reach shallow water," gasped Danny.

7—Laur... gangsters were arm... question. As the crew of the ...in towards the island, an amazing ...swordfish which had chased the pals to ...water and smashed its great snout into the heli..., lurched wildly under the terrific blow. Then, with its ti..., the machine crashed into the sea.

...e and Dingo stood for a moment, dumbfounded. Then ...led, "C'mon, Dingo! We've gotta get the crew out of ...never swim in those heavy flying clothes." As the ...through the shallows Danny saw his chance. ...quickly as possible, Bob," he ordered. "I'll ...his knife, the lad crept up behind Laura ...bonds. "Don't make a sound," he ...ay!"

...Danny managed to keep his speedy craft just ahead of the ...sh until they reached the shallows round the island, where ...Bob raced for cover. Round a headland the helicopter was ...its way slowly along the shore. The last thing the pals ...was to be seen by the helicopter's crew. "It looks as if ...spotted Jake and Dingo," hissed Danny.

6—On the shore there was plenty of cover to be had in thick tropical vegetation which covered the island. Never exposing themselves to the helicopter, the friends made their way through the thick undergrowth, guided by the deep roar of the helicopter's engine. Suddenly, they heard shouts ahead of them. "That sounds like Jake and Dingo," muttered Danny. Stealthily, the pair moved forward until they were only yards from the crooks.

9—In a few moments the girl was free. "Quickly now," said Danny. "Follow me through the jungle. And run like the wind. We've only minutes to get away from this island alive." The boy and girl raced away at top speed smashing their way through tangled foliage. Anxiously, Danny kept glancing over his shoulder for signs of pursuit, but it seemed they had a good start.

10—At last they reached the shore where the Iron Fish lay beached. Bob Hartley was there straining with all his might to get the Iron Fish into the water. Swiftly, the exhausted Laura and Danny clambered into the Fish. "O.K., Bob! One last push!" said Danny. The pilot waded out, pushing the Fish until it floated. Then he squeezed into the cockpit beside Laura.

1—Working in cramped conditions, Danny had difficulty in handling the controls. However, the lad managed to start the Fish and set it on course for Rio. For the first time since they had set out to trail the kidnappers Bob and Danny felt safe. "If the weather holds, it'll be plain sailing from now on, Bob," said Danny. Bob Hartley chuckled. "And those toughs are going to find that island a pretty safe prison. It'll be a simple job for the police to pick them up, now." Steadily, the Fish pushed on across the calm waters, carrying the fugitives towards the coast. "Let's hope we make land before dark," said Bob anxiously.

12—After some hours, Danny spotted a whisp of ship's smoke above the horizon, and turned the Iron Fish towards it. Swiftly, the vessel loomed larger until its look-out spotted the Fish. Tired but happy, Laura and her rescuers were helped aboard the vessel, a Brazilian warship, which made full speed for Rio when the captain heard Danny's story. The news of the rescue was passed on by radio. When the warship finally docked, Laura's father and a battery of newspaper men were waiting to welcome her. The joyous look on Laura's face was enough to convince Bob and Danny that all the dangers they had passed through had been well worth while.

THE END.

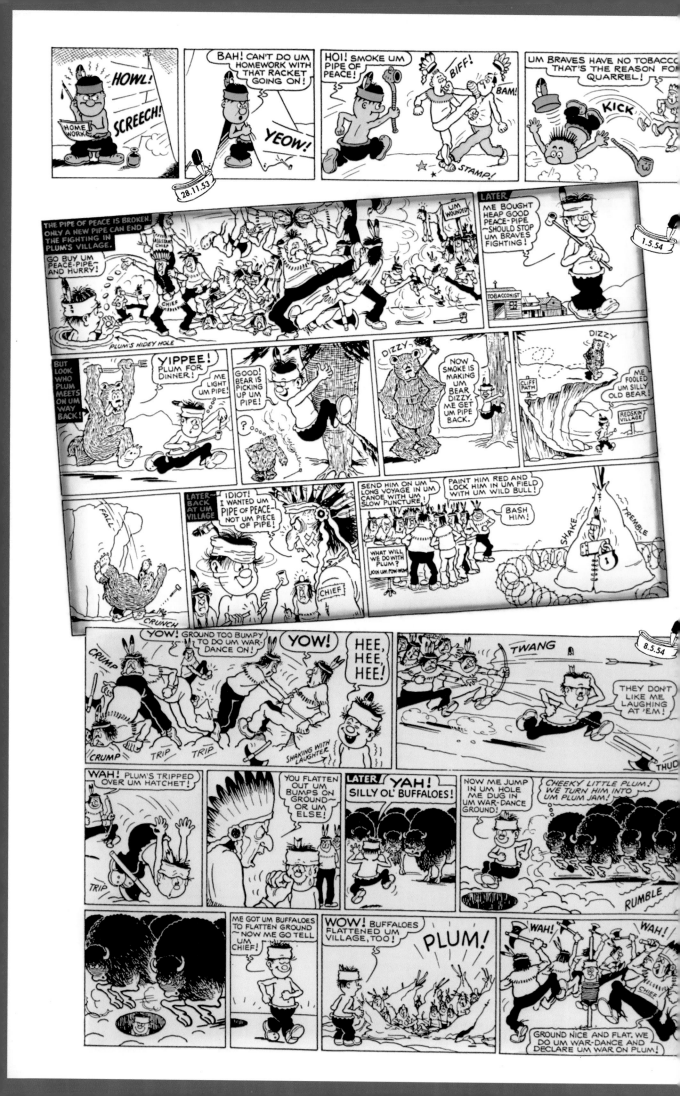

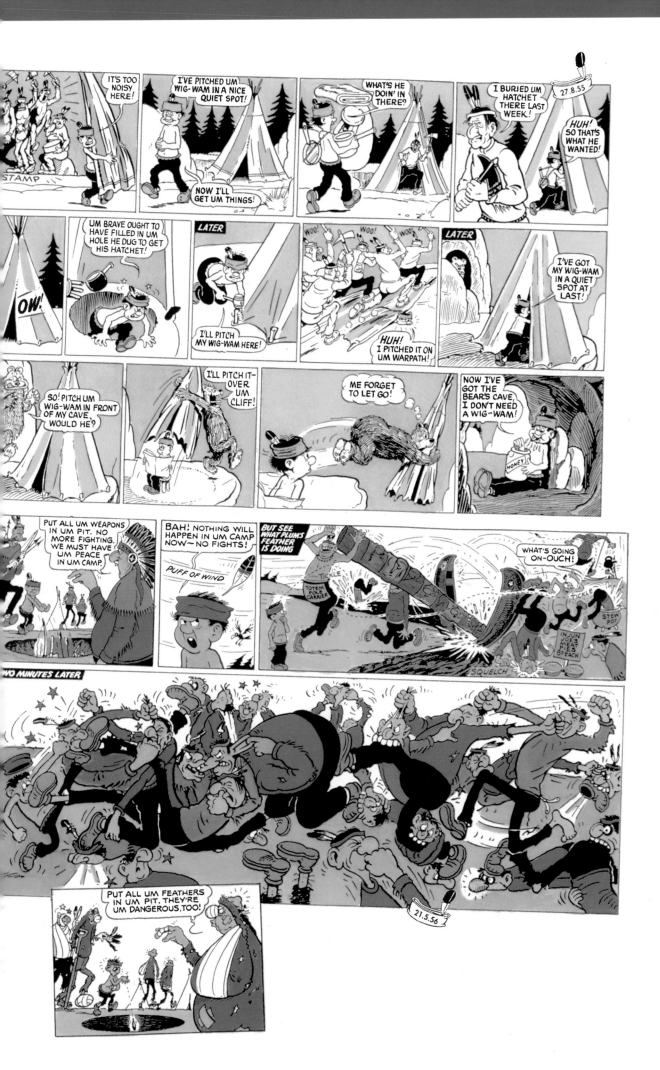

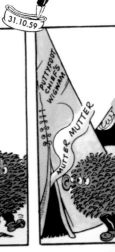
31.10.59

I WANT YOU TO DISGUISE YOURSELF AND INFILTRATE INTO UM PUTTYFOOT CAMP AND SEE WHAT YOU CAN LEARN!

THAT BUSH CAMOUFLAGE WILL GET YOU INTO UM PUTTYFOOT CAMP WITHOUT BEING SPOTTED!

YOU COULD HAVE PICKED UM BETTER BUSH ~ THIS ONE'S FULL OF EARWIGS!

PUTTYFOOT SENTRY

TO UM PUTTYFOOT CAMP 50 YARDS

¼ MILE PER HOUR

PUTTYFOOT CHIEF'S WIGWAM

MUTTER MUTTER

MUNCH

THE ROTTEN OL' PUTTYFEET ARE CHOPPING DOWN MY TALL TREE TO MAKE A TOTEM POLE!

I'LL HAVE TO MOVE MY NEST TO THIS NICE LITTLE BUSH!

HOW EMBARASSING!

GROOH! SPLUTTER! UM BIRD'S STUFFING UM WORMS INTO MY MOUTH!

?

THEN ALONG COMES UM PUTTYFOOT GARDENER ~

I'M OFF!

INSECT SPRAY

MANURE

CHOP CHOP CHOP

THEN ~

I'LL GET ME THAT BUCK RABBIT FOR DINNER!

BLAM

?

THAT LAST VOLLEY WAS UM BIT TOO CLOSE! I'LL MOVE BACK UM BIT!

UM JUMPING BUSH?!!

BLAM

UM SPY!

SPIFLICATE HIM!

WELL, PLUM? WHAT DID YOU LEARN?

I LEARNT NEVER TO SNEAK INTO UM PUTTYFOOT CAMP DISGUISED AS UM BUSH!

PLUM'S CINEMA

SHOWING TODAY "THE BATTLE AT BOULDER CANYON"

FILL THEM REDSKINS WITH LEAD, MEN!

HURRAH FOR THE COWBOYS!

BOULDER CANYON

SUDDENLY, HELP ARRIVES FOR THE OUT-NUMBERED REDSKINS — FROM THE "ONE AND NINES"!

GURR!

...EN THE "TWO AND SIXPENNY" SEATS ...ND THE COWBOYS A HAND!

MY FIRE ARROW WILL FIX THAT WAGON!

AFTER THE SHOW —

EXIT

IT'S ALWAYS THE SAME WHEN I SHOW A WESTERN FILM! THE AUDIENCE GETS CARRIED AWAY — AND MY SCREEN IS RUINED!

NEXT DAY —

I'LL PAINT A WHITE SCREEN ON THIS CLIFF FACE!

WHITE WASH

...THAT NIGHT THE FILM IS ...N OUT OF DOORS!

BUT — THE SAME THING HAPPENS —

CRACK

LOOK OUT! OUR BULLETS HAVE STARTED AN AVALANCHE!

...L?

THEY ALWAYS GET "CARRIED AWAY" AT A WESTERN FILM!

28.11.59

DAYS LATER — AFTER THE AUDIENCE RECOVERS —

WANTED MAN WITH BROADEST CHEST IN THE WEST APPLY LITTLE PLUM AT THE CINEMA

WARNING TO PATRONS DON'T START A-SHOOTIN' AT THE SCREEN — IT'S LIABLE TO START A-SHOOTIN' BACK!

LOOK! THERE'S NOT A SIGN OF A HAIR. MY CHIN'S AS BALD AS AN EGG.

No bristles on his chin and no hair on his head! These can't be pictures of Desperate Dan! —

THE NEW CACTUSVILLE BARBER SHOP

DESPERATE DAN NEVER COMES TO ME FOR A HAIRCUT. HE ALWAYS CUTS HIS OWN HAIR, DRAT HIM!

TRY MY HAIR RESTORER

NO NEED FOR WIGS

HE NEVER COMES FOR A SHAVE EITHER. HE USES SANDPAPER—

NO NEED FOR WIGS

—THEN FINISHES OFF WITH A BLOWLAMP!

NO NEED FOR WIGS

LATER THERE'S DAN SUNBATHING. NOW'S MY CHANCE TO MAKE HIM A CUSTOMER OF MINE.

I'LL RUB HIM WITH HAIR REMOVER. THEN HE'LL WANT TO BUY A BOTTLE OF HAIR RESTORER.

HAIR REMOVER

AN HOUR LATER 13.7.54 WHAT'S HAPPENED TO ME? MY SKIN'S GONE SOFT AND ALL MY WHISKERS HAVE FALLEN OUT!

SHUCKS! I MUSTN'T LET ANYONE SEE ME WITHOUT BRISTLES ON MY CHIN. PEOPLE MIGHT THINK I'VE TURNED INTO A SOFTY.

THAT NIGHT COO! SAY, UNCLE DAN, YOUR CHIN'S AS WHITE AS A RICE PUDDING. ALL YOUR BRISTLES ARE GONE! YOU DO LOOK SOFT.

I SHAVE A BLOW YESTERD

NEXT MORNING LOOK! THERE'S NOT A SIGN OF A HAIR. MY CHIN'S AS BALD AS AN EGG.

THAT MUST HAVE BEEN A SPECIALLY HOT BLOWLAMP YOU USED, YESTERDAY. IT'S BURNT UP THE HAIR ROOTS. HERE— UNCLE DAN, WE CAN MAKE MONEY OUT OF THIS!

DESPERATE DAN'S HAIRCUT SHOP LET DAN SHAVE YOU AND YOU'LL NEVER NEED TO SHAVE AGAIN.

LET US MAKE YOUR CHIN LIKE — DAN'S — IT'S HAIRLESS FEEL IT AND SEE.

IN DAN'S SHOP SHAVES—
BY BLOWLAMP—10c
BY FILE — 25c
BY SAND PAPER — 50c

COME IN, GENTLEMEN

IT'S ONLY YOU TOFFS WHO ARE SHAVED BY SANDPAPER. THE CHARGE IS 50 CENTS.

THOSE WHO CAN'T AFFORD 50 CENTS GET AS GOOD A SHAVE WITH A FILE FOR 25 CENTS!

THE REAL TOUGH GUYS WITH NO SWANK LIKE THE BLOWLAMP. LOVELY SHAVE. ONLY COSTS 10 CENTS!

WOW! OUCH HOWL!

LATER QUEER! I THOUGHT I WOULD GET DESPERATE DAN AS A CUSTOMER. BUT INSTEAD HE'S STARTED A BARBER SHOP OF HIS OWN.

BARBER TRY MY HAIR RESTORER NO NEED FOR WIGS

DESPERATE DAN'S HAIR-CUT SHOP

NEXT MORNING AH! GOOD OH! HAIRS A APPEARING ON MY CHIN AGAIN—EVEN A BLOWLAMP OR WHA IT WAS CAN'T STOP MY WHISKERS GRO FOR LONG.

I'M GLAD, UNCLE DAN. YOU LOOKED A PROPER CISSY WITHOUT THEM!

D.WATKINS

*- or can they? Read these
ages from July 1954 and
pril 1952 to get the whole
airy stories!*

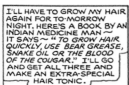

PANSY POTTER

1—Old Wizard Touch has come to town. Now Mary wears a worried frown. She has a lamb as white as snow, and Wizard Touch has made it grow. Still Pansy says she'll do her best to fix old Wizard Touch—the pest. But Wizard Touch, to her surprise, increases Joe Grasshopper's size. Off goes our tough wee lass full speed upon a most amazing steed.

2—Cries Wizard Touch, " Hooray! Hooray! That's Pansy well out of my way." Joe spies the window of the Zoo. He bucks and Pansy whizzes through. Bang! Crash! She feels a bit upset. But she will fool the Wizard yet. She'll do the very best she can. A tiger cub gives her a plan. She starts to cover it with glue. Oho! What is she going to do?

3—She sticks wool on the glue. That's smart. And very soon the fun will start. The Wizard sees the " lamb." Oho! With his queer wand he makes it grow. The " lamb's " a giant tiger now. The Wizard scoots off shouting, "Wow!" He leaves his wand, and straightaway our Pansy cures the lamb. Hooray!

A milkman and a blacksmith battling a horde of Vikings! Unbelievable? Well the story appeared in The Dandy back in 1952, so judge for yourselves! It was described as "The First Viking Invasion since the days of Alfred the Great!" The title — "Fighting Forkbeard — the Sea Wolf From Long Ago"!

A WILD battle song rang out over the waters of the northern sea. Great oars splashed, keeping time with the song; and the men at the oars were big and wild and hairy men, wearing iron helmets and shirts of mail. They were like the Vikings who brought fire and the sword to the coasts of Britain a thousand years ago — and their boat was a Viking boat! "What land is that, Forkbeard?" asked the foremost oarsman; and the big fork-bearded man in the bows waved his battleaxe. "One of the isles of Britain," he said. "And soon it will be Forkbeard's island!"

2 — The Viking galley was heading into a sandy bay. High up on cliffs beyond the beach stood the village of Graysham, and on outskirts of the village was Ben Bolt's blacksmith shop. It was ea morning, but big Ben Bolt was busy. Even in the year 1951 there v plenty of work for a village smith. Then, above the ring of hammer, he heard a shout. "Hi, Ben! Big Ben!" yelled the voice, Archie Thoms, the milkboy, came tearing furiously along on his bi "Look! There's a Viking ship out there — a real one, like the drawi in my history book!"

3 — Big Ben ran to look at the long galley and its strange crew. "Why, it is a Viking ship!" he gasped. "But there are no Vikings nowadays. It must be some kind of a stunt." Stunt or not, the local coastguard and two policemen were already on their way to the beach. They arrived as the ship grounded on the sand. Forkbeard bounded ashore, roaring his battle-cry, and other strange men from the sea were to be seen splashing after him.

4 — The coastguard and the policemen hesitated when the fierce-e sea wolves came up with a rush, with shields advanced, and bat axes whirling. There was no escape for the three men when Vikings ringed them in. Meanwhile, other Vikings were dragg their ship up the beach. And that was the scene when Big Ben and milkboy arrived at the cliff-top. "Gosh! What are they going to d Captain Green?" gasped Archie.

5 — Even as they watched, Captain Green drew something from his pocket. It was only an official paper, but the move was enough to make Forkbeard leap forward with swinging axe. The flat of the blade struck the Captain's head. As he dropped, the two bobbies were likewise felled to the ground. Big Ben's grip on his big hammer tightened. "What's the big idea?" he muttered, and started to climb down to the beach. As Ben slid down, Archie saw two Vikings run towards the cliff.

6 — The Vikings hid behind a couple of boulders, and Archie Th realised with a thrill of fear that they were lying in wait for blacksmith. What should he do? Should he shout a warning to Ben? No! Ben would look up, and his attention would be right of danger ahead of him. Archie looked around in desperation, and eye lit upon the milk bottles on his bike. He seized one and hurl downwards with quick and desperate aim. Ben was now only y away from the ambush.

– Archie's aim was truer than he had dared to hope. The bottle ~~ere~~tered on the helmet of the Viking who was about to strike. Big ~~en~~ whirled, saw the reeling Viking, and instantly swung his hammer ~~n a~~ two-handed swipe that felled the man like a log. The other Viking ~~cam~~e at the smith with flashing axe. Clang! Ben's hammer parried the ~~blo~~w, and the force of the Viking's swing spun the stranger half-~~rou~~nd. The young blacksmith was fighting for his life now, and he showed no mercy. Down came the hammer on the horned helmet, and down went the second Viking. A howl of fury went up from the other sea wolves. Forkbeard had seen the ambush go wrong, and now he thirsted for vengeance. "Ho! A foe worthy of my steel!" he bellowed. "Come, sea wolves! I would have a closer look at this enemy of the strong arm." In a surging, roaring wave, the Vikings charged up the beach towards the lone blacksmith.

– Big Ben caught his breath at the terrible sight of flashing steel in ~~the~~ hands of so many wolf-like men. Then he did the wisest thing! He ~~scr~~ambled in mad haste to the top of the cliff. The Vikings were hot ~~on~~ his heels, but once at the top, Big Ben had the advantage. He ~~turn~~ed to meet them, his sledge-hammer swinging. One Viking went ~~do~~wn. The next swing was aimed at Forkbeard, and the Viking leader ~~onl~~y saved himself by throwing up his shield. Even so, the heavy ~~blo~~w sent him flying.

9 — Big Ben kept the hammer swinging, and in his powerful grip it felled half a dozen Vikings, one after the other. The invaders were beaten back. They retreated to the foot of the cliff and gathered in a scowling, whispering group. Then came the second attack. Ben stood ready to hold his ground, but Archie suddenly nudged his arm. "Watch out, Ben! They're coming up further along the cliff as well." Ben saw at once that he had no chance against a two-pronged attack. On came the Vikings.

~~1~~0 — Ben remembered the bike. "Quick, Archie. Tip out your milk ~~b~~ottles. We'll need that carrier." Archie ditched his load and Ben Bolt ~~s~~wung a leg over the bike. "Hop up in front, Archie!" he said, "and ~~h~~old on to my hammer!" Then, wobbling a little until he picked up ~~sp~~eed, Ben cycled away along the cliff path. A great howl of rage ~~w~~ent up from the Vikings, and a flying axe hurtled narrowly past his ~~h~~ead. Big Ben kept going!

11 — When Ben next glanced back, he was out of danger. The warriors were not even looking in his direction. Fighting Forkbeard and his Vikings stood gaping at the white milk bottles, and it was long ere one daring sea wolf risked handling them. Then the warriors stood in a bunch, gingerly passing the bottles round — and not one of them dared to open a single bottle! So began Britain's first Viking invasion for over a thousand years.

the Bash Street Kids

WHEN THE KIDS ARRIVE AT SCHOOL ONE MORNING~

I WANT THREE VOLUNTEERS TO COLLECT A POSTER FROM THE PRINTERS ~ YOU, YOU AND YOU!

MAD, COMPLETELY MAD!

WE'VE BEEN SENT BY THE COMMANDER OF THE BESIEGED FORT TO GET HELP FROM THE FIFTH CAVALRY. LOOK OUT FOR APACHES, MEN!

AT THE PRINTER'S

AH, YES, HERE'S THE POSTER FOR YOUR TEACHER!

10.10.59

PRINTER / PRINTERS

I'M LATE FOR SCHOOL. I'LL HAVE TO HURRY ~ OW!

BONK

YOU BASH ST. BONEHEADS! WHY DON'T YOU STAY IN YOUR OWN PART OF TOWN? OUTA MY WAY!

STAMP STAMP STAMP STAMP

CRUMP!

LET'S GET OUT OF MINNIE THE MINX'S WAY BEFORE SHE CRIPPLES US FOR LIFE!

YOU BUCKLED MY BIKE AND BENT MY BOKO, YOU BLITHERING, BLOCK~HEADED BASH ST. BABOONS!

OOOOH HOLLY HEDGE!

5 MINUTES LATER ~ THE KIDS ARE TAKING A SHORT-CUT ACROSS THE SLUDGE ST. SCHOOL PLAYING FIELD.

ERK~HERE COME THOSE BULLIES FROM SLUDGE ST. FIFTH FORM ~ THEY'LL TAKE OUR POSTER OFF US!

SHOVE IT THRO' THIS KNOT-HOLE QUICK!

I'LL TAKE THIS RARE EGG TO THE SCHOOL COLLECTION ~ BET I GET A PRIZE FOR IT!

THAT'S THE POSTER SHOVED THROUGH THE KNOT-HOLE, THE SLUDGE ST. LOT WON'T SPOT IT NOW!

SPLAT

ROTTERS! SQUELCHING MY EGG WITH YOUR ROTTEN POSTER!

CRUNCH

BONK

HELLO, YOU UGLY BASH ST. TOADS ~ WHAT'S THIS YOU'VE GOT ~ A ROLL OF PAPER? HMM, I THINK WE'LL HAVE IT FOR MAKING PAPER AEROPLANES!

YOU'LL HAVE TO FIGHT US FOR IT!

CRUMBS, THIS IS LIKE HITTING A LUMP OF CONCRETE!

ACHE

BONK BONK BONK

THUD

GASP

CRUMP

CLASS 2 D.

HERE'S THE POSTER, TEACHER! WHAT A JOB WE HAD GETTING IT HERE SAFELY!

NO DOUBT YOU'LL BE INTERESTED TO SEE WHAT'S ON THE POSTER!

FIGHTING IS STRICTLY FORBIDDEN PENALTIES JELLY NOSE~ 100 LINES THICK EAR~ 200 LINES BLACK EYE~ WHACKING

SUFFERING CATFISH WOULD YOU BELIEVE IT

Desperate Dan's nephew, Danny, and his niece, Katey, met for the very first time, back in February 1957.

How many things on this page are not seen or not
allowed, today? Er, just about everything!
So, please, readers, do NOT copy anything
you see on this page from a 1958 Beano!

This Biffo
the Bear page
has almost no
clues as to when it might have been drawn —
a bear, a cabinet, lots of water and not much else.
But the title of this book is a clue, so you can
'drawer' your own conclusion! Is it from the
'70s, '40s, '60s, or '80s?

ANSWER —
For those who haven't looked at the title of this book,
the page is from the '50s — 24th August 1957, to be exact!

JENNY PENNY

This charmingly evil little lass could be spotted in the pages of The Dandy between 1954 and 1955, with appearances in The Dandy Books of 1956 and 1957.

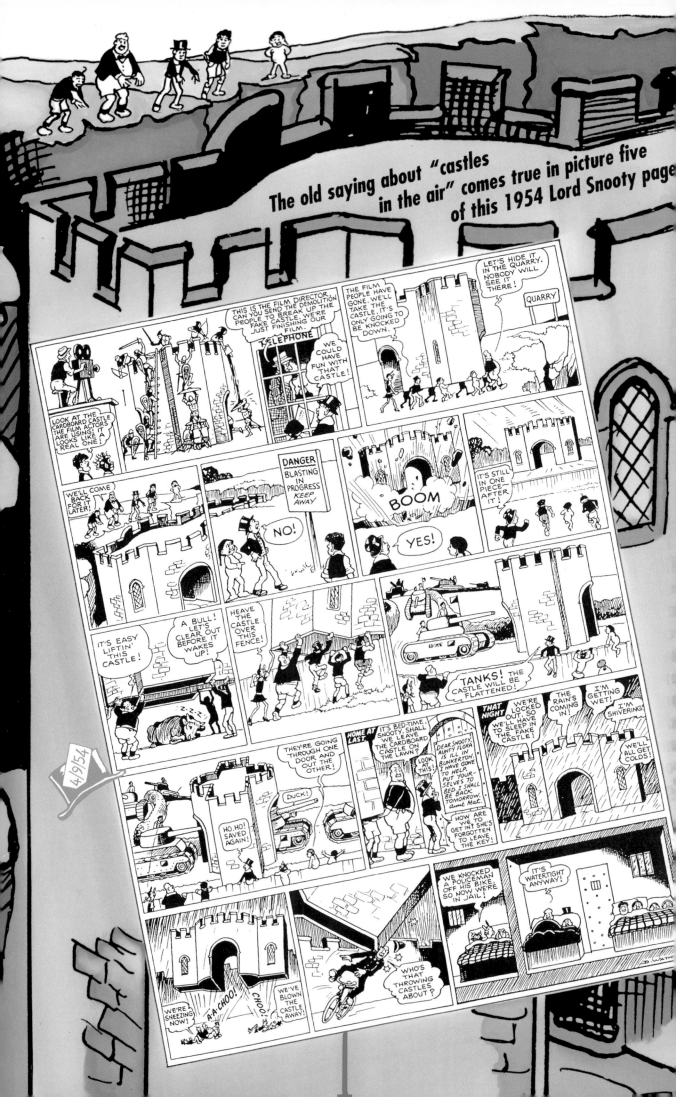

Roger the Dodger has been a firm favourite in The Beano for fifty years, since his first appearance in 1953. It should have been 51 years, but somehow he dodged the pages of The Beano between April 1960 and April 1961! Turn over and you'll see one of his favourite dodges.

ROGER the DODGER

OOPS! THE WINCH WASN'T SECURED! THE PERISHIN' CABLE'S JUST WINDING OFF THE DRUM! I HAVEN'T MOVED AN INCH YET!

THIS LOOKS RATHER 'DODGY', READERS! PLEASE DO NOT COPY ROGER!

SLACK

BRUM-M

RM-M

R-R-R

R

PHUT

BUT AT THE TOP OF THE HILL, THE CABLE RUNS OUT—

NO MORE ON THE DRUM!

LP! IT'S RUNNING OWNHILL AND I CAN'T STOP IT!

LOWER DOWN THE HILL—

YOUR GO, WILLIE.

RUMBLE

MY BEST NEW MARBLES —GROUND TO POWDER!

GANGWAY!

CRUNCH

WHOOSH!

CRASH!

WHEN THAT BOY OF MINE COMES HOME —I'LL FIX HIM!

BUT ROGER WON'T BE HOME FOR A LONG TIME, FOLKS—

THERE'S A MILE OF IT TO RELAY!

GASP!

DON'T ARGUE WITH ME, ROGER. BRING A BUCKET OF COAL WHEN YOU'RE TOLD!

I'LL HAVE TO PUT A STOP TO THIS COAL-CARRYING ONCE AND FOR ALL!

THIS IS IT. FOLKS! I'M GOING TO 'ACCIDENTALLY' TRIP ON PURPOSE, AND SPILL THE COAL ON THE NEW RUG.

OOPS! SORRY, DAD!

THAT'S ALL RIGHT, ROGER. IT'S ALL GONE ON THE FIRE. NOW YOU'LL HAVE TO BRING SOME MORE!

BAH! I SHOULD HAVE TIMED THAT TRIP TWO PACES SOONER!

LATER—

THANK YOU, ROGER! NOW GO AND WASH.

MUTTER-MUTTER-MUTTER!

NOW YOU CAN CHOP SOME FIREWOOD!

I'LL TURN THE WIRELESS ON, SO THAT I CAN'T HEAR HIS COMPLAINTS!

DAD!-GASP!WHEEZE!- THIS AXE IS BLUNT! OUCH! DAD! I'VE HIT MY THUMB! CAN YOU HEAR ME, DAD?-DAD! DAD!

I CAN'T HEAR HIM. GOOD DODGE, THIS!

BLAH! BLAH! BLAH!

HALF AN HOUR LATER—

OH, ROGER! BEFORE YOU CHOP ANY MORE LOGS, RUN AND TELL THE SWEEP TO CALL. THE CHIMNEY IS SMOKING.

DODGE HATCHING!

LET ME SEE NOW! NO SWEEP—NO FIRE! NO FIRE—NO WOOD-CHOPPING OR COAL-CARRYING! M-M-M-M!

SO—AT THE SWEEP'S—

'MORNING, MR SWEEP! OUR CHIMNEY NEEDS SWEEPING, AND DAD SAID ~ TELL OLD BALDY-HEAD BROWN TO DO IT!' THAT MEANS YOU!

YOUR DAD SAID WHAT?

J. BROWN CHIMNEY SWEEP

YOU CAN GO HOME AND TELL YOUR DAD THAT I WOULDN'T SWEEP HIS PESKY CHIMNEY— EVEN IF IT WAS THE LAST PESKY CHIMNEY ON EARTH!

IT'LL BE A PLEASURE!

AT HOME—ROGER TELLS ALL— WELL—ALMOST ALL!

SO HE WON'T SWEEP OUR CHIMNEY, EH?

LOOK HERE, BROWN! WHAT'S THE IDEA OF REFUSING TO SWEEP MY CHIMNEY?

GOSH! I DIDN'T COUNT ON DAD PHONING.

BLAH! BLAH! BLAH! PESKY SON OF YOURS! BAH!-AND-BLAH! BLAH! BLAH! — AND THAT'S FINAL!

— AND WHO CALLED THE SWEEP A BALDY-HEAD?

I DID! HERE'S YOUR SLIPPER, DAD!

I DON'T MISS THE FIRE. THIS WARMS ME UP!

GOLLY! A DODGER'S WORK IS NEVER DONE!

LET'S GO TO THE CIRCUS, SWOTTY.

WE CAN'T~FOR THREE REASONS. ONE~WE GOTTA GO TO SCHOOL~ TWO~THERE'LL BE CROWDS GOIN'! AND, THREE~WE'RE BROKE!

CIRCUS

RIGHT! FIRST, WE'LL DODGE SCHOOL!

MY I-I SEE PRO WITHO

SNATCH

AT THE RAILWAY STATION—

STATION

WHICH WAY IS THE CIRCUS?

RIGHT, SWOTTY! MEET ME ON THE COMMON WITH YOUR TANDEM IN HALF AN HOUR.

NO IDEA, CHUM.

GOING TO GET RID OF THE CROWDS NOW, EH?

TO THE CIRCUS

LOOK! THAT BOY'S GOING TO THE CIRCUS.

HE MUST BE A GUIDE. FOLLOW HIM.

TO THE CIRCUS

ON THE COMMON—

THIS IS WHERE WE PART COMPANY, FOLKS.

TO THE CIRCUS

JAB!

HE'S TURNED THE SIGN ROUND.

HA! HA! SMASHIN' DODGE THAT, ROGER.

TWISTER! RO

OH! EASY YOU HO

Item of interest for fans —
K. Reid, the name on the junk
collector's car in picture 5
above, was the 'Roger' artist
during the 1950s.

WAIT A MINUTE! ENERGETIC MUGS ARE HANDY CHAPS TO HAVE AROUND! I'LL HAVE A WORD WITH 'EM!

ROGER DOES—AND A DODGE IS BORN!

DON'T FORGET YOUR PROMISE, ROGER! FAIR SHARES FOR ALL WHEN YOU REACH THE TOP!

NOW YOU'RE FOR IT, YOU DODGING TWISTER!

OUCH!

BUMP!

BUT, JUST AT THAT MOMENT—

DING-DONG!

QUICK, TUBBY! THAT'S THE SCHOOL BELL. WE'LL BE LATE!

WHEW! SAVED BY THE BELL!

PLUNDERER! SCALLYWAG! THIS IS ONE OF MY PRIZE PIPPINS THE ONLY ONES IN THE DISTRICT! I'D RECOGNISE THEM ANYWHERE!

GOSH! TEACHER'S THE NEW OWNER OF THAT ORCHARD.

AFTER SCHOOL—

NO! ROGER HASN'T TAKEN UP GYMNASTICS. IT'S JUST THAT HE'S BEEN STANDING IN A CORNER ALL AFTERNOON AND HIS FEET ARE KILLING HIM!

TWINGE

IN THE HOUSE
SOMETHING'S INTERFERING WITH YOUR RECEPTION, DAN. I CAN'T GET ANY PICTURES.

NOW WHAT'S CAUSING THAT?

OH, I SEE! — THAT MOUNTAIN PEAK'S IN THE WAY.

OH, WELL, I'LL SOON FIX THAT!

OFF I GO WITH A FEW OF MY TOUGH TOOLS.

NOW I START BY BORING A HOLE WITH MY BRACE AND BIT.

AT THE OTHER SIDE
I'LL CUT THE LAST CHUNK OUT WITH MY TOUGH SAW.

SAW

THAT'S IT! OUT GOES THE CHUNK!

HOME AGAIN

'50s TELE-WATCHING — THE DESPERATE DAN WAY!

This Desperate Dan story received a warm reception from Dandy readers in 1953!

EVERYTHING'S HUNKY-DORY NOW!

LATER
WHAT'S WRONG NOW? THE PICTURE'S ALL WAVY. I'LL GO OUTSIDE AND SEE WHAT'S HAPPENING.

AH! MRS BRIGGS HAS GOT AN ELECTRIC SWEEP. HO! LET ME DO THE CHIMNEY-SWEEPING FOR YOU. IT'S SPOILING MY T.V. RECEPTION.

BUZZ

ALL RIGHT, I'LL LET YOU DO IT, DAN!

THANKS, MRS BRIGGS. I'LL JUST **BLOW** THE CHIMNEY CLEAN!

16.5.53

HOWL! MY WASHING! COVERED WITH SOOT!

YOU BIG PALOOKAH! YOU'LL DO MY WASHING ALL OVER AGAIN!

O.K., MRS BRIGGS. I'LL WASH IT AS WHITE AS SNOW!

I'VE GOT ME A FINE WASH-TUB. SO NOW I CAN SETTLE DOWN TO WASH AND WATCH T.V.

DRINK, HORSEY, DRINK.

THE TROUGH'S GONE!

D. WATKINS

Minnie the Minx began her reign of terror in December 1953 — the last of the stalwarts of that year who are still in the Beano comic today. She first appeared as a bit of a beanopole — sorry, beanpole — but as the '50s progressed, she came to be drawn much shorter, although the laughs were just as long!

The very first Bash Street Kids story wasn't actually called that — the original title was "WHEN THE BELL RINGS", and the first of these was in the Beano issue dated 13.2.54. This changed to "THE BASH STREET KIDS" in Beano issue dated 17.11.56 and has remained as the title up to the present day. Throughout the Bash Street Kids' early years it was never made clear exactly how many kids there were — the maximum number stated in one story (see following picture) was 16 kids! Not all were named, however. One long-standing title had 11 named kids including Teddy the teddy boy, then when the title was changed (see illustration) there were 12 rear ends!

Also, just to confuse things, the "WIZARD" comic carried Bash Street Kids stories in text format in 1955, giving their town and teacher proper names, which the Beano had never done. The kids' names were "expanded" (e.g. "Smiffy" was identified as James Smith). An example of this appears elsewhere in the book.

It wasn't until the early '60s that changes to the Kids "settled down" and they became the ones we know today.

TEACHER'S READING A STORY

"LAND AHOY!" YELLED THE MAN IN THE CROW'S NEST. "LAND AHOY!"

PLEASE, SIR, THAT'S RIDICULOUS, SIR. HOW COULD A MAN BE IN A CROW'S NEST?

SIT DOWN, BLOT, AND I'LL TELL YOU WHY!

THE CROW'S NEST IS......

A SUDDEN THOUGHT STRIKES TEACHER

I'VE JUST REMEMBERED!

I HOPE I'M IN TIME!

TEACHER ARRIVES HOME

TOO LATE! I LEFT THE GAS BURNING UNDER A POT OF PORRIDGE THIS MORNING. OH, DEAR!

SILLY OL' TEACHER RUNNING OFF LIKE THAT, AND THAT DAFT STORY HE WAS READING ABOUT A MAN IN A CROW'S NEST. PAH!

WE'LL SEE IF IT'S POSSIBLE YOU, SMIFFY, HOP UP THAT TREE AN' SIT IN THAT NEST!

SMIFFY HAS A TRY!

NOW TEACHER'S ON HIS WAY BACK TO SCHOOL

WHAT ARE YOU KIDS DOING HERE AND WHAT'S THAT SILLY BOY DOING UP THAT TREE?

LOOK OUT BOY!

'SNO USE! CAN'T BE DONE!

TEACHER'S AFTER US. FOLLOW ME!

HE'S NUTS!

WHAT DOES HE THINK WE ARE?

WE'LL REFUSE TO LISTEN TO THESE SILLY STORIES TEACHER READS IN SCHOOL. WE'LL TELL HIM IT'S IMPOSSIBLE FOR A MAN TO BE IN A CROW'S NEST!

IT'S DAFT STUFF!

IT'S THOSE BASH ST. KIDS! THEY'RE HIDING IN THE CROW'S NEST UP THERE!

THE BASH STREET KIDS

THE KIDS HAVE GONE NUTS ON EARTH SATELLITES EVER SINCE THE RUSSIANS SENT THEIRS UP A COUPLE OF MONTHS AGO~ I CAN'T STAND IT ANY LONGER!

BLEEP! BLEEP! BLEEP! BLEEP!

THAT NIGHT~

I'VE HEARD THAT SCIENTISTS ARE PLANNING TO SEND UP MONKEYS IN EARTH SATELLITES NEXT~ WELL, I'LL DO SOME MIDNIGHT SWOTTING~

LATEST ROCKET TECHNIQUE

~AND BUILD MYSELF AN EARTH SATELLITE. I'LL SEND UP MY OWN LOT OF MONKEYS IN IT. (YOU KNOW WHO!) THAT'LL GET RID OF THEM FOR GOOD!

ONE WEEK LATER~

HELLO, MONKEYS~ I MEAN CHILDREN! AS A TREAT I'M GOING TO LET YOU WATCH THE LAUNCHING OF MY NEW PRIVATE EARTH SATELLITE!

SMASHIN'! GOOD OL' TEACHER!

BLEEP! BLEEP! BLEEP!

STEP INSIDE THIS OBSERVATION PLATFORM, KIDS. YOU'LL GET A SUPER VIEW OF THE LAUNCHING FROM IT!

BLEEP! BLEEP! BLEEP!

HEH, HEH! THAT'S NO OBSERVATION CHAMBER~ THAT'S THE SATELLITE!

CLANG!

SIZZ

FIRE!

YIPPEE! WE'RE GOING UP IN A SATELLITE! BLEEP! BLEEP! BLEEP!

OHH! I FORGOT TO TAKE THE MOORING ROPE OFF AND THE ANCHOR'S CAUGHT ON THE CHIMNEY OF MY HOUSE!

SWOOSH

THE MOORING ROPE CAUGHT ON THE CHIMNEY IS MAKING THE SATELLITE SPIN ROUND AND ROUND TEACHER'S HOUSE!

BLEEP! BLEEP! BLEEP! BLEEP!

BEDTIME! THE SATELLITE IS STILL SPINNING ROUND TEACHER'S HOUSE!

BLEEP! BLEEP! BLEEP!

CHEEP CHEEP

SMIFFY ALWAYS DOES THINGS WRONG

DRAT IT! I'M WORSE OFF THAN WHEN I STARTED~ NOW I CAN'T GET ANY SLEEP, SLEEP, SLEEP!

14.12.57

THE BASH STREET KIDS

"HIYA, SQUARES!"

"I'M TAKING MY ROCK 'N' ROLL RECORDS TO SCHOOL TO PLAY THEM ON THE SCHOOL RECORD PLAYER!"

AND SO IN SCHOOL

ROCK-ITTY-ROCK ROCK!

JUMP AN' ROCK ROCK AN' ROCK

BUT CUT IT OUT!

"CHEEKY BRAT! USING THE SCHOOL RECORD PLAYER FOR NASTY ROCK'N'ROLL MUSIC! I'LL GO AND LOCK IT UP!"

"THESE ARE THE CLASSICAL RECORDS FOR THE LECTURE THAT YOUR TEACHER IS GIVING TO MY CHAMBER MUSIC SOCIETY TONIGHT!"

"QUICK, TEDDY! WE'LL SWAP YOUR ROCK'N'ROLL RECORDS FOR THESE OL' MINUET RECORDS BEFORE TEACHER GETS BACK!"

17TH CENTURY MUSIC

THAT EVENING AT THE LECTURE

1.3.58

SENT!

REAL GONE

COME AN' ROCK ROCK, ROCK, MY PRETTY BABY!

BOOM BOOM

"MUST GET THIS RECORD OFF QUICK— OW!"

SNAP

STOP!

LET'S ROCK AN' JUMP WO-O-O-AH!

"I WON'T HAVE YOU LOWERING THE TONE OF MY SOCIETY!"

WHOP

20.6.59

CLANG CLANG CLANG CLANG CLANG

...YTIME'S OVER—...ME TO COME...R LESSONS...OAH!! THEY...EN'T TAKING... BIT OF NOTICE!

GO GET 'EM, LEO!

TEE~HEE! LEO'S DRIVING THE KIDS INTO THE CLASSROOM!

SNARL

...M PECKISH. ...LL HAVE... SWEET!

THAT SOUNDS LIKE A PAPER WRAPPER BEING TAKEN OFF A SWEET!

RUSTLE

??

GROWL!

SNATCH

GOOD DOG, LEO! YOU CAN HELP YOURSELF TO THE SWEETS FOR CATCHING THAT FAT GLUTTON EATING IN CLASS!

SLURP! CHOMP!

AT GYM

UP THE ROPES, CHILDREN!

LOOK, NO MUSCLES!

AW! WE'RE TOO TIRED FOR THAT!

GROWL

...D...O...!...T...MBING!

THAT NIGHT

THIS BOOK ON VENTRILOQUISM MY DAD GOT FROM THE LIBRARY WILL HELP FIX THAT DOG. I'LL STUDY IT IN BED TONIGHT!

HOW TO BE A VENTRI~LOQUIST

NEXT DAY

I SAY, TEACHER. I'VE GOT A SCHOOL BOARD MEETING ON IN TEN MINUTES' TIME. WILL YOU CORRECT THESE HOMEWORK ESSAYS FOR ME?

NOW'S MY CHANCE!

CORRECT 'EM YOURSELF, YOU FAT BLADDER OF LARD!

I'LL TEACH YOU NOT TO INSULT YOUR HEADMASTER. I'LL DOCK YOUR WAGES!

...R! WHO CALLED ...HE HEAD ...MES?

I DID, YOU SKINNY WEED!

DANNY'S THROWING HIS VOICE

HEAD! IT WAS THIS DOG THAT INSULTED YOU, NOT ME!

HEAD

GO ON, SAY SOMETHING, LEO, TELL THE HEAD WHAT YOU TOLD ME— SPEAK UP YOU STUPID ANIMAL! SAY SOMETHING!

SILENT

COMING IN HERE EXPECTING ME TO BELIEVE A COCK AND BULL STORY ABOUT A TALKING DOG! TAKE THAT!

BASH ST. SCHOOL

SUPER! TEACHER'S SENT THAT FOUR~LEGGED MENACE AWAY FOR GOOD!

D

the BASH STREET KIDS

BASH ST. SCHOOL IS ENTERING A PERCUSSION BAND IN THE LOCAL MUSICAL FESTIVAL!

GROAN!

WE START REHEARSALS NOW. HERE ARE YOUR INSTRUMENTS!

FIRST REHEARSAL

DONK

SQUELCH

CLANG

BAP!

YOU HOOLIGANS! YOU'VE RUINED THE INSTRUMENTS. NOW YOU'VE NO CHANCE OF WINNING THE FIRST PRIZE — A FREE FEED!

CASTANETS

THERE'S ONLY ONE THING FOR IT, KIDS. WE'LL HAVE TO FIND SOME MORE INSTRUMENTS!

AND SO—

Z-Z-Z

BRING THE BOTTLES OF MILK IN, ALBERT!

RIGHT, DEAR — ERK!

I'VE BORROWED YOUR MILK BOTTLES. I'VE EMPTIED THE MILK INTO THIS NICE CLEAN BUCKET

PIG BUCKET

CRASH!

CLANG!

BANG!

GOODNESS ME, WHAT IS THAT TERRIBLE NOISE?

IT'S THE BASH ST. KIDS "CONCUSSION" BAND.

CRASH

RATTLE!

BONG

CLANK

CHING

MILK

UNFORTUNATELY, THE JUDGES AT THE FESTIVAL DON'T APPROVE.

THIS BAND IS BANNED!

AND NOW TEACHER'S GOT HIS OWN PERCUSSION BAND!

I'LL TEACH YOU NOT TO RUIN THE GOOD NAME OF THE SCHOOL!

AWW!

EEEK!

OWOW!

YOWLK!

HOWL!

21.11.59

YES, it's the Bash Street Kids, but NO, it's not the BEANO!
Read the explanation on the page opposite.

...may surprise you to know that the Bash Street Kids didn't only appear in The Beano! Back in '55, boys' paper The Wizard carried a series of text stories by the title "Bash Street School" in ...ich the gang appeared. Those stories contained some 'tweaks' of the names, addresses and even ... pupils that attended. Were those minor changes a good idea? Judge for yourself by reading the story below, from June 4th, 1955.

BASH STREET SCHOOL

...N'T think I've told you about "Beaky" Parret, our ...ing Gym teacher, writes Sidney Pye of Class II.C, ...treet Junior Secondary Modern School, in Northport. ...aky" comes twice a week to Bash Street to take the ...s of Northport — that's us — for gym. During the rest ...week, Beaky is at Winsor Crescent, a posh Grammar ...l on the other side of town.

...looks down on us, and never gets tired of telling us ...a shower of stiffs we are.

...t week, going to school with Smiffy, I discussed ways ...eans for taking a rise out of Beaky.

...e trouble with the big lug," I said, "is that he really ...we're not as good as the Winsor lot."

...ell, they play rugby, so we can't wallop them at ...," Smiffy pointed out. "And the cricket team is too ...o play us."

...mehow, we've got to get a crack at the toffs and lick ... at something," I said. "In the meantime, let's ...ntrate on Beaky."

...r gym is at the other side of the playground from the ...l. When we went over that morning, Beaky was ...ere around. Then we spotted him, panting along Bash ... on his bike.

...ere's a chance, chaps," I rapped to the gang. "By the ...Beaky goes to the staffroom and gets over here, we ...o quite a bit of 'doctoring' in the gym."

... slipped inside and got to work.

...ew minutes later, Beaky appeared and told us to ...e. We got into our running shorts — those who had ... — and nipped into the gym.

...et down two mats," snapped Beaky to Gasbag and me. ... bring out the basketball stands. We'll have a spot of ...ork, then we'll finish up with a game of basket-ball." ...was a programme that suited the japes well. As a ...r of fact, Beaky nearly always does the same thing, ...e'd had a good idea what to doctor.

... formed into a long line, and at the very end of the line ... the gang — Gasbag Jones, Wilfred, Fatty Brown, ...y, Death's Head Danny Morgan, and your pal, Sid. We ... good reason for waiting till the end.

...un up," commanded Beaky, "and do a forward roll on ...at, rising sharply to your feet afterwards."

... line started to run. One after another, the lads of II.C ... their forward roll. Fourteen had gone over before my ...made their rolls, and if you'd watched closely, you'd ...noticed that we rolled as close to the outside edge of ...at as possible.

...ter more mat exercises, we ran round the gym for a bit. ...haps started to sweat.

...en I noticed Tweetie Wilson, the class sneak, starting ...iggle. More lads began to wriggle, till soon nearly the ...e of II.C were wriggling about like snakes on a hot ...

...alt!" yelled Beaky. "What's the meaning of this?" ...ease, sir," gasped Tweetie, "my back feels very itchy." ...o does mine," came a chorus from the rest of the lads. ...en, suddenly, Beaky himself began to fidget. He stood ...e foot, then on the other. Then he began to hop about ...ad. Soon he looked as if he was dancing the Highland

...arry on, boys," he puffed, and disappeared in the ...ion of the little staffroom beside the gym door.

...hen he went out, I laughed till I thought I'd burst. The ...tching-powder routine has been worked in every ...ol since itching-powder was invented, but it still strikes ... funny. We'd filled Beaky's gym shoes with it. Then, ... we had some left, we thought we'd jape the class, ...ing that all the toadies, including Tweetie Wilson, ...d get the biggest dose of powder. They always rush to ...ont, so we dusted the mat in the middle.

...hen Beaky came back, we saw that he'd changed his ...s. He ordered us to bring out the basket-ball stands. ...e started a game of basket-ball, but nobody seemed to ...le to score. Time and again, sure goals bounced out of ...et. Beaky got wilder and wilder.

...he boys of Winsor Crescent could give you lessons on ... to shoot!" he narked. "Come here and I'll ...onstrate."

...e gathered round. Beaky is a big bloke, over six feet, ...ll he has to do to score is to stretch up and plop the ball ... he net.

... did that. The ball bounced back. He tried again. Same ...t. He got wild and began pitching the ball up again and

...en Beaky cooled down and had one of the stands tilted ...ard. He soon found out the cause of the bad shooting. ...sbag had carefully criss-crossed black thread over the

top of the net. From below the thread was invisible, but it kept the ball out just the same.

We'd made a mug out of the chief snob, Beaky. But he had the last word.

"You're a crowd of numbskulls!" he bellowed. "The boys of Winsor Crescent could teach you manners — and they would whack you at sport, too, you inferior ruffians!"

"Can you fix a cricket match?" I said, like a shot.

"No!" said Beaky decidedly. "I wouldn't have anything to do with showing you up. Besides, the Winsor Crescent lads pick their company carefully."

We were wild, but there was nothing we could do, until, after the bell rang, I had a Pye brainstorm.

"We'll run in their Inter-schools Relay race on Saturday," I announced. "Then we'll make Parret eat his words."

"How can we do that?" said Smiffy. "We aren't invited, and if we tried to gatecrash we'd be pitched out on our ears."

"We'll ambush the Cliffhill College team," I said. "They're that posh mob who caught Bash Street boys once, and covered them all over with boot blacking, remember? We owe them one for that. With their togs and borrowed strips, we can sneak into the race."

"We'll have to win," pointed out Gasbag.

"We will," I said grimly. "We've got the speed to do it. Today is Monday. We'll train hard every night, and practice baton-changing till Saturday."

SATURDAY found us trained to a hair, and waiting at the railway station for the visiting teams to arrive. First to come was the team from the very posh place, Cliffhill College.

"Hello, chaps," I said, going forward and speaking as posh as I could. "This is a reception committee to take you to the Winsor Crescent sports ground."

"Frightfully decent of you," said the tallest of the four. "We weren't sure of the way, though we intended to follow the map you sent."

That solved one thing that had puzzled us — and had seemed a snag in our plan — why no Winsor Crescent boys had appeared. They'd sent full directions to their visitors instead.

Our reception committee numbered eight, the usual six plus Bulgy Buchan and Foghorn Reid. They were members of the relay team, since Fatty was too fat, Wilfred too small, and Smiffy and Gasbag only ran when chased by a wild bull.

With eight against four, the ambush was a sure thing. Passing along the street that Fatty lives in, we suddenly grabbed them, two to each Cliffhill boy, and hustled them into Fatty's shed. It was done so quickly that before they realised it they were inside.

"Hand over your bags," I rapped.

"There's nothing valuable in them," whined one of the college boys.

"We'll judge that," I growled.

The poor, spineless saps handed over their bags without a murmur. We grabbed their caps, and decided to do without the ties. Whipping out, we locked the shed.

"So far, so good," said Bulgy Buchan, our class brain, and a very fine sportsman, too. "Now for the sports."

Winsor Crescent had very fine playing fields — not like the mudheap we play football on, or the Public Park we use for cricket. Round the field, tents had been put up, and when I handed over the competitors' tickets I had found in one of the Cliffhill bags, we were taken to one of the tents to change.

For the occasion we had all borrowed spikes for running. We didn't have any of our own, but Wilf's brother is Secretary of the local harriers. After a week's training with them we felt pretty confident.

It wasn't long before we'd dressed ourselves in the flashy silk singlets of Cliffhill College, and shortly afterwards, our four non-runners appeared at the back of the tent. They'd sneaked in under the hedge round the ground. We gave them our ordinary clothes, packed in the Cliffhill lads' bags, so that we could make a snappy getaway.

We hadn't long to wait. Soon the loudspeaker called for "Runners in the Under-Fifteen Schools Relay". We crept out and made for the starting-line.

Then we saw a big snag. Beaky Parret was acting as starter. If he saw us, the game was up.

Three of us, however, moved to the change-over places. The distance was four-hundred and forty yards, with each runner doing one hundred and ten yards.

Bulgy Buchan was the first runner, and he kept well back till the last second. Then he pretended to blow his nose as they went to their marks. Beaky didn't notice him.

"Bang!" Beaky's gun went off, and so did the sprinters. Coming to the first change-over, there was nothing in the race at all. I won't bore you by naming the other schools. All we were interested in was Winsor Crescent, and I'm sure you feel the same way.

At the change-over, Bulgy slapped the baton into Danny Morgan's hand, and Danny went like the wind. He led by a about a yard as he pushed the baton into Foghorn Reid's fingers. It was a perfect chance.

Third man for Winsor Crescent was a lanky bird. He gained on Foghorn, and amid a din like a Cup Final he passed him.

But as I grabbed the baton for the last lap, I knew I just had to do it! Out of the corner of my eyes I could see Beaky Parret waving his arms, and I knew we'd been spotted. If we didn't win we'd be the laughing-stock of Northport.

I went for the tape like a scalded cat. There were blokes on both sides of me — then there was nobody. I broke the tape, and the chaps told me later I had a two-yard lead at the end.

Of course, Winsor College masters tried to grab us, but we dived for the hedge, and got clear. Then we headed back to Fatty's shed to let the prisoners loose.

"There'll be trouble on Monday," warned Gasbag, as we wandered off down Bash Street.

But we didn't care. I had an idea that the Head wouldn't wallop us quite so hard as usual. For a heading in the Evening Sports paper read — "Bash Street School Pirates sail home to Victory."

Hands up all readers who thought Desperate Dan never strayed from the pages of The Dandy?

he Boyhood OF DESPERATE DAN

ESPERATE DAN didn't get much schooling
when he was young because the tough folk of
bstone didn't set much store on book learning.
e age of twelve Dan weighed fourteen stone ten
ds and he could wrestle a bull with one hand
nd his back, but he couldn't count.

an's education really started the day his Paw
him to dig a well eighteen feet deep in the
en.

ater was short that year on account of Dan
ng up the logs for winter. He sawed so fast that
gs kept bursting into flames, finally setting the
e woodpile on fire, and the water had to be
to put out the blaze.

ou'll have to dig a new well tomorrow, son,"
Dan's Paw. "Go down about eighteen feet."
kay, Paw," said Dan.

e next day Paw went off to work in the stone
ry as usual, but when he came home to dinner
w a huge mountain of earth in the garden and
le hole a mine shaft beside it.

e hole went down so far that Paw couldn't see
ottom, so he dropped a heavy rock down to
out how deep it was. He listened for a while,
heard a heavy thud, followed by a roar like a
ano blowing its top.

ho dropped that pesky pebble?" Dan's voice
peted up from the hole with such force that it
i Paw's hat off.

's me, son," Paw called down. "Did I hurt
?"

o, Paw," bawled back Dan, "but it's sure lucky
ght the rock on my head otherwise it might
busted the shovel in two."

w gazed down the hole again.

on," he said, "I thought I said for you to sink
well eighteen feet. How come you're down
ty?"

Vell, Paw," admitted Dan, "I ain't figured out
far down eighteen feet is yet. I never learned to
nt more'n ten."

w gazed at the deep hole, then at the huge
ntain of earth, and sighed.

on," he decided, "you gotta have schoolin'."
nd that was how Desperate Dan's schooldays
y began.

HE schoolmarm at Tombstone was Calamity Liz
Laramie, who weighed twelve stones, chewed
ed rope because she couldn't stand the taste of
cco and was so handy with a six-gun that she
ld ring the school bell with a bullet at five
dred yards, which partly accounted for the
ol inspector giving Tombstone such a wide
h.

alamity Liz had trouble with Dan right from the
. This was because the school desks had been
t for ordinary-sized youngsters, while Dan at
time stood five feet ten and a quarter inches in
socks, and measured fifty-five inches round the
st.

The desk split in halves when Dan tried to
squeeze his knees under it.

"I'm sure sorry to be puttin' you to this trouble,
ma'am," said Dan to the angry teacher, "but I guess
I'll have to make me a desk that'll fit me."

And he borrowed an axe and nipped out to the
woods, where he hacked down one of the Never-
Bender Trees, which only grow around Tombstone
and are so tough that the folk use them for making
bullet-proof doors for their shacks.

It would have taken a lumberjack a couple of
hours to saw through a Never-Bender Tree, but Dan
just gave it a few belts with his axe, then threw his
weight against it, snapping it off short.

Dan carried it back to the school playground on
his shoulder, sawed it into planks and set to work to
make himself a desk. He didn't have any hammer,
but at twelve years old he had learned how to punch
nails in with his bare fist, so he soon got the job
done.

But when he tried to get the desks into the schoolhouse he ran into more trouble. It was too big to go
through the doorway.

"The pesky doorway ain't wide enough, ma'am,"
he said to Calamity Liz, and he wedged himself
between the doorposts and heaved them apart.

There was a loud cracking noise. Dan widened
the doorway considerably, but then the school roof
started falling in. There were howls of panic from
the other kids and Dan had to stand and hold the
roof up while they scampered to safety.

Calamity Liz was getting mighty mad by this time
and her shooting hand was itching. But she didn't
go for her gun because there were strict rules against
plugging new kids on their first day at school.

"Sure reckon I deserve a larrupin' for causing you
so much inconvenience, ma'am," said Dan humbly,
when he had managed to get the roof propped up
again.

"Sure reckon you do," yelled Calamity Liz.
"Bend over! This is gonna hurt me more than it is
you."

She was right there. When she brought the cane
down on Dan's seat, it snapped in halves and
Calamity Liz flapped her fist and let out a screech as
if she'd been stung by one of the Skewer-Skeeter
Flies from the Ozone Swamps who have stings like
red-hot porcupine quills.

"Quit the ticklin', ma'am," urged Dan, "and get
on with the larrupin'. It ain't no more'n I deserve."

Calamity Liz got a new cane, but that broke, too,
and she got madder and madder until she had
broken every cane in the school. Then she got the
big pole she used for lifting down the maps and

belted Dan across the seat with it. But the pole just
snapped like the canes and Calamity Liz had to give
up.

"I'll punish you a different way," she yelled.
"While the other kids have their half-holiday this
afternoon you'll stay in and write spellings."

So that afternoon Dan sat in the empty
schoolhouse with pencil and paper. He wasn't much
of a hand at writing and he pressed too hard on the
pencil, with the result that it broke in halves.

After he had broken a dozen pencils, Dan decided
to try a pen. He jabbed it into the ink-pot, then heard
a crack and felt something trickling down his leg.
He's stabbed the pen right through the bottom of the
pot and all the ink ran out.

Dan scratched his head blankly for a bit, then he
noticed the blackboard. He decided to write his
spellings on that.

But the board was covered with sums, so he had
to rub it clean first. But he rubbed so hard that
smoke started rising and the blackboard burst into
flames.

When it was four o'clock and Calamity Liz came
back to see how Dan was getting on, she found him
sitting on the school step with a slab of stone from
the quarry. He was hacking out his spellings with a
chisel.

Dan had to do his homework on a paving stone, using a hammer
and chisel as a pencil.

"Ain't no other way I could write the pesky words
down, ma'am," he said.

Calamity Liz had got to figuring by this time that
Dan was going to be the problem child of the
school. So she went round to see Paw next day and
told him she reckoned Dan was kinda big for school
and she reckoned he would learn to count quicker in
other ways, like counting the cows, for instance.

So Dan was sent round to all the ranches and told
to work out the number of head of cattle in each
herd. Dan soon learned to do this by counting all the
legs and dividing the total by four, which worked
fine except once when he made the total come to
176 cows because he had counted in the rancher's
legs by mistake.

After that Dan was set to counting the apples in a
neighbour's orchard. He was there all the afternoon
and when the neighbour turned up, the orchard was
stripped as bare as a bald head.

"Where's all my pesky apples?" howled the
neighbour.

"Well, I didn't want to run the risk of counting the
same apples twice," explained Dan, "so I just
popped each one in my mouth as I counted it off."

Dan's Paw got a shock when the neighbour sent
him a bill for fifteen hundredweight of apples.

"Ain't you got stomach-ache, eatin' all them
apples, son?" Paw asked Dan.

"Naw," said Dan. "I figured them apples might be
sour, Paw, so I stopped at another plantation on the
way and ate fifteen hundredweight of sugar melons
to be on the safe side."

Paw scratched his head at that, especially when he
got the bill for the sugar melons and learned that
Dan was planning to visit the Tombstone Pie
Factory the next day to count the pies.

"Son," said Paw, "I reckon you've been eddicated
enough. From now on you're packin' in this
schoolin'."

Dan didn't mind, but he always looked back to
that time and said his schooldays were the best days
of his life.

RED RORY
of the
EAGLES

29.9.51

RED RORY MACPHERSON woke with a start as the harsh warning cry of an eagle sounded overhead.

It was the year 1747. Little more than a year before, the Highland Army under Bonnie Prince Charlie had been defeated at Culloden. Now garrisons of red-coated soldiers were stationed everywhere in the Highlands to keep order.

Rory had been driven from his home and forced to flee to the hills, in company with others of the Macpherson Clan. The clansmen had dared to disobey a Royal Proclamation which forbade the wearing of tartan.

The boy had vowed that he would never give up wearing the kilt which had belonged to his father, who had died fighting at Culloden.

Two great golden eagles were circling low over his head. The birds were Rory's friends. He called them Flame and Fury. He had trained them since they were young and now they seemed to understand every word he said. They had been wheeling over his head, keeping watch whilst he slept, ready to warn him of danger. And now — the danger had come.

Cautiously Rory sat up. He strained his ears to listen for any unusual sound.

Soon he heard the deep-throated baying of the Redcoats' bloodhounds.

He began to wriggle his way cautiously through the heather. Soon he reached a spot from where he could look down the ben.

There were half a dozen dogs on the leash and at least a score of soldiers turning out in a long, red line right across the lower slopes.

Then, Rory saw one of the Redcoats stop in his tracks and point into the air above the spot where Rory lay hiding. The soldiers had seen Flame and Fury hovering just above Rory's head!

A Redcoat officer gave the order and the dogs were slipped from their leashes. They leapt forward up the slopes. Behind the animals the men broke into a shambling run.

Rory darted away, heading for the river. Once across the water, he could throw the dogs off the scent.

Above his head the eagles wheeled. They would not desert him even in the greatest danger.

But Rory faltered as a sudden dread thought struck him. The river was too deep and wide and swift-flowing for a man to swim across. The Redcoats would trap him there on the edge of the rocky bank.

Rebel's Leap

THEN Rory remembered the Rebel's Leap.

As a young boy he had heard the story of how a hunted Macpherson had climbed to the top of a jagged rock at a narrow part of the river, and in a desperate effort had managed to leap across to the opposite bank. The leap was nothing short of miraculous, and Rory knew that not one man in a thousand could make that leap. Yet it was his only hope of escape.

Behind him the baying of the dogs sounded ever louder.

Grimly determined, Rory sped away, in the direction of the Rebel's Leap.

Desperately he pulled himself on to the top of the rock that towered beside the river, and lay for a moment, gasping for breath. But he couldn't afford to wait. He could see the dogs now, bounding over the heather towards him.

He dragged himself to his feet. The top of the rock was flat, and about a dozen feet across.

Rory retreated as far as he could to the edge of the rock. He glanced upwards for a moment and saw that Flame, the eagle, was wheeling just over his head.

From below came the crack of a musket, and a ball hit the rock a few inches below his feet.

Then Rory ran like the wind and leapt into space.

The very instant he jumped, he knew that he had failed. The distance was too great. He was doomed to fall into the raging river below.

Then a shadow came over his head and a rush of wind ruffled his flaming red hair. Flame was gliding down just before his face.

The great golden eagle had realised his danger and was coming to help. In desperation Rory's hand shot out and clutched the hooked talons. Flame beat her mighty wings in a gallant attempt to rise, checking Rory's fall just long enough to carry him to safety.

Now Rory was over the rock on the far side of the Rebel's Leap. He let go and fell face forward on the rock.

But Rory was not yet out of danger. The m... dogs could not cross the river — but bullets... As he lay there on the rock, there came the c... musket fire, and balls chipped the stone... hand.

He scrambled to his feet and began to c... way up the slope on the farthest side.

Then to his ears came an unexpected so... was the well-loved sound of the bagpipes.

Rory lifted his eyes to the skyline. There... his head, wild and defiant, the figure of... strode up and down. He was deliberately st... on the skyline, trying to draw the soldie... towards his own gaunt figure. For Callum th... also wore a kilt.

The Redcoats, with hoarse cries of anger,... their muskets at the figure on the skyline an... the rocks re-echoed to the crash of their rapi...

The diversion enabled Rory to scramble... disappear from sight down the other side of t...

Rory did not see Callum stumble and... forward on to his knees, hit by a musket b... glanced from the flat top of a rock. Presen... sound of the pipe music died away.

By that time Rory and his eagles were... hidden.

Soon, Rory came out of cover to seek out... and thank him for saving his life.

A hundred yards away he could see C... Something was wrong! His pipes were un... arm and he was walking away from Rory... dozen times he stumbled and nearly fell. Onc... saw the piper pass a shaking hand uncertain... his eyes.

The boy's face grew white, for he su... realised that Callum was heading straight... edge of a deep corrie.

The Blind Piper

Rory gasped an order to the eagles ov... They understood at once, and went racing a... force Callum away from danger. The grea... were just too late.

With a cry that echoed around the hills,... went over the edge of the cliff.

Rory darted forward and looked down o... edge.

Thirty feet below was a four-foot wide led... just below the ledge a bush grew from the... the rock. Callum the Piper was clinging desp... to the bush.

"Hold on, Callum man," called Rory.

The drop to the ledge was sheer... impossible to climb down at that point. Rory... have to find another way farther along the... wall.

With a flutter of wings Flame settled besid... — and the youngster looked at the bird.

Rapidly he began to give the grea... instructions in a language that the eagle unde...

As Rory ran for the easier way down to the... Flame dropped like a stone down the face... rock to hover like a great shadow over the pi...

Callum's strength was ebbing fast.

Then he felt Flame's powerful talons take... on his thick homespun shirt. He felt himsel... upwards, and he used the last ounce of his... strength to pull himself up with the help of th...

At last Callum's fingers curled over the rim... ledge and Flame's great wings beat the air... sought to lift Callum's body on to the shelf c...

It was there that Rory found him when at... finished his climb. The piper was lying st... rigid, his bloodstained face to the sky.

"You're injured, Callum!" cried Rory.

"Aye, lad, I am." The piper's voice was... and very weary. "A musket ball glanced from... and struck me square in the face."

Gently the youngster wiped the blood... Callum's face. Sightless eyes stared up at hir...

"I — I can't see!" whispered Callum.

Rory sat very still. His friend was blind! It... drawing the fire from Rory that Callum had l... eyesight.

"Listen, Callum," said Rory, and laid a h... his friend's arm. "There is a doctor who li... Perth. He was a very good friend of my fathe... is skilful in treating eyes. We must go to him...

Rory allowed Callum to rest for a while... helped the injured man to climb the steep side... corrie to the level ground above.

There Rory bathed the piper's face with... from a mountain steam. Refreshed, Callum d... plaid about him, and the two friends strode of... South and the unknown dangers that lurked t...

e were seven series featuring Rory and his eagles. The first was
y text, then the Highland laddie flew back to the pages of the
o in 1952 in picture story format for the next ten years. The
mples shown on these two pages are from September 1951 and
ember 1958.

It is the summer of 1746 and many of the clan chiefs who took part in the '45 Rebellion have escaped the English troops and left Scotland to find sanctuary in France. Red Rory McPherson with his pet eagles, Flame and Fury, has done much to help fugitive chieftains reach safety.

58

One day while on the North-West coast of Scotland, Rory spotted a man swimming ashore from a French ship, and dragging a sea-chest on a raft.

Suspicious, Rory sent Flame and Fury to harry the man.

screeching eagles swooped towards their prey.

Displaying the strength of ten, the man swung the heavy raft, keeping the eagles at bay.

Rory drew his dirk and jabbed it against the man's ribs. "One more move and you're as good as dead," he hissed.

The lad forced the big man to open the sea-chest.

om the chest the man drew out a kilt. Rory sped in astonishment. The Redcoats had forbidden the wearing of this garment.

Rory lowered his dirk. "My apologies," he said. "You're one of us!" Swiftly, the man dressed himself in the kilt.

The man whose name was Black Duncan told Rory why he had landed on this remote stretch of coast. Duncan and his chieftain had escaped the clutches of the English troops and reached France some weeks before. However, the chieftain's wife and two children were still in Scotland. It was Duncan's task to take them safely to his chief.

"I'd like to help you in your mission," said Rory. "You're welcome, lad," replied Black Duncan, grasping Rory's hand warmly.

KAT and KANARY

'50s ANIMAL WELFARE — THE DESPERATE DAN WAY!

A snake eating cow pie; a lion in a hammock; a crocodile on the mantelpiece . . . what else could this be but a Desperate Dan story, from 1956!

A Tonic - With Happy [...]er Effects!

THE BEANO

NOV 10th, 1956.

2D

EVERY THURSDAY

Back in November 1956, Biffo thought that the latest Beano Book was great stuff, so if you turn to the next few pages you'll find all his favourites that he mentions on the cover.

GROCER

BIFFO THE BEAR

I'LL SIT ON THIS BARREL AND READ THIS YEAR'S "BEANO BOOK." IT'S SUPER!

TREACLE

GROCER

HO! HO! PRINCE WHOOPEE KNOCKS OUT THE BUNG OF A TREACLE BARREL...

TREACLE

GROCER

... AND PEOPLE GET THEIR FEET STUCK IN TREACLE—WHAT A LAUGH!

GOSH! ROGER THE DODGER IS ON THE RUN WITH ARROWS WHISTLING PAST HIS HEAD!

ARCHERY CLUB

BOOM!

CIRCUS

THE HORSE THAT JACK BUILT IS A GREAT YARN—"A CANNON BALL HURTLED TOWARDS HIM AT POINT-BLANK RANGE."

ZOO

NOW FOR SAMSON AND THE SHIPWRECKED CIRCUS—WOW! "A GIGANTIC SNAKE WAS CRAWLING FROM A TREE TOWARDS SAMSON—"

PHEW! I GOT THIS ESCAPING PYTHON IN THE NICK OF TIME!

PHEW! SAMSON GOT IT IN THE NICK OF TIME!

CLUMSY!

IT SLIPPED!

ICE FACTORY

THE BIRD BOY IS A GOOD STORY, TOO—"SUDDENLY, WITHOUT WARNING, JAGGED LUMPS OF ICE BEGAN TO FALL. KELVIN PULLED UP SHARPLY!" PHEW!

GREAT STUFF! WHY DON'T SOME OF THESE EXCITING ADVENTURES EVER HAPPEN TO ME?

ROGER the DODGER

STEP INTO THESE, ROGER! YOU'RE GOING TO HIKE ~ AND LIKE IT!

TA VERY MUCH ~ I DON'T THINK!

—AND I WOULDN'T TRY ANY DODGES ON THIS TRIP, M'LAD! I'LL CATCH YOU UP LATER ON MY BIKE, AND THERE'LL BE A NICE SQUARE MEAL READY WHEN WE GET BACK!

HUH!

'SFUNNY! I'M LEAVIN' A TRAIL OF ARROWS BEHIND ME!

?

SO THAT'S HIS GAME! A RUBBER ARROW-STAMP FIXED TO EACH SOLE!

ROGER WORKS A COUNTER DODGE

HOW ABOUT SWOPPING SHOES, MISTER?

DON'T MIND IF I DO, MATEY!

HOME

BOY! WHAT A DODGE!

DAD'LL NEVER LEARN! HE OUGHT TO KNOW BY NOW HIS SON'S THE KING OF THE DODGERS!

I JUST HAVE TO FOLLOW THE TRAIL OF ARROWS TO FIND ROGER.

BUT AT THE END OF THE TRAIL—

?

HOWLING HORRORS! I'VE BEEN FOLLOWING A TRAMP! I'VE BEEN DODGERED!

AND THEN—

HARD LUCK, MATEY! LOOKS AS IF YOU'RE IN FOR A LONG WALK!

BANG.

ONE FIVE-MILE STAGGER LATER—

HI, DAD! I SAVED YOU SOME OF THE SQUARE MEAL ~ A NICE SQUARE BISCUIT!

GRRR!

GR-R-R-R-R! GR-R-R-R-R!

OUTSIDE—GR-R-R!

IF YOU WANT TO KNOW WHERE ROGER IS ~ JUST FOLLOW THE ARROWS!

DAD'S NO SPORTSMAN! HE'LL NEVER ADMIT TO BEING OUT-DODGERED!

ZING

WHEE-EEEE

PLOP

10.11.56

TREACLE

THE HORSE THAT JACK BUILT

10—" Prepare to repel boarders !" Jack leapt on to his Horse as the ships clashed bulwark to bulwark and a horde of cut-throats swarmed from the rigging of the pirate ship. Jack pressed a saddle button and one of the Horse's forelegs shot out like an expanding telescope, knocking a pirate from the rigging. At the same time he pressed another button to raise himself high in the air on the saddle. From this vantage point he fought furiously with the belaying pin. Slowly the pirates were beaten off.

11—The pirate ship slid swiftly away from the Golden Hawk. But the pirate chief was not giving up the fight. He tried other tactics. BOOM! BOOM! At point-blank range his cannon raked the merchantman in a fierce broadside. Boom!

12—A cannonball ripped into the bulwarks Jack's side. Splinters flew, and in a moment was menacing the ship. Attempts to douse it w unsuccessful. The flames spread. The ship doomed! "Abandon ship !" roared the Cap

THE SHIPWRECKED CIRCUS

...ially, with the roots cracking like ...e chums disentangled the parachute from the pilot. "My name's Jeff Wilkins. I've got a plantation on ...was starting out on a tour of them when a storm blew up, and——" ...startled gasp. From the hole left by the tree roots, a gigantic snake was crawling!

5—Never had the chums seen such a gigantic creature! For years it must have been lurking in tunnels and caverns under the island, and the felling of the tree had opened an escape hole. As the snake crawled into the open Samson seized the parachute which Wilkins had unbuckled.

6—Moving at tremendous speed the snake slid towards the chums. But Samson was ready. He held the parachute up so that the wind, blowing towards the monster, filled the silk like a huge balloon. Suddenly he released it and it was whisked forward over the great snake's ugly head.

The BIRD BOY

A HUGE white bird wheeled in the chill air above the gleaming, icy wastes of the Antarctic. I an albatross, and it carried a queer burden. A young boy, clad in a single garment of p feathers, was clinging to its scaly legs, his body swaying to the slow, graceful wing-beats. H the Bird Boy had lived most of his life in the Antarctic. Now he and his strange pet, the albatross, were preparing to land on the whaling ship that lay on the vast white sea. But it sea of ice, for the winter had come quickly, and the narrow strait in which the ship had been p had turned to ice overnight, locking the ship in its grip. The whaler was the Berga, and Jim and his crew were Kelvin's friends. As the albatross glided down, Kelvin saw somethin brought a flash of anger to his eyes. One of the whaling men was aiming his rifle at a baby seal.

......ivin quickly. ......tement at Harper's Bay." So ......m was mushing the huskies swiftly over the i with Jim Richards lashed to the dog-sled.

6—Soon they reached the edge of the ice and K steered the huskies along the icy shore below tall cliffs overhung with ice cornices. Suddenly, without warning, jagged lumps of ice, loosened by the vibration set up by the sled, began to fall.

Kelvin pulled up sharply, but he was too late to save the big lead-dog. Sharp ice sheared through the traces, and the dog was hurled into the icy sea. Immediately a huge, killer whale rolled on the surface nearby and moved towards the dog.

Science-fiction comes to Lord Snooty, in 1954! It's the world's first 'microwave oven'!

PROFESSOR SCREWTOP'S SENT US A MECHANICAL COOK. THIS BOOK OF INSTRUCTIONS TELLS US HOW TO PUT IT TOGETHER.

NOW I'LL JUST SPEAK INTO THE MICROPHONE ...... MECHANICAL COOK, WE WANT BAKED SOLE, CHIPS, FRUIT, TRIFLE AND MORE CHIPS!

I'LL PUT IN THE INGREDIENTS.

LATER
SOMETHING'S GONE WRONG! THE FOOD HAS COME OUT JUST AS WE PUT IT IN.

WE'LL GIVE THE COOK ANOTHER CHANCE. MAKE US A FRUIT PIE THIS TIME, AND HURRY UP!

RIGHT THIS TIME ~ AND NO NONSENSE! IT'S A PIE!

GROOGH! IT'S TERRIBLE! UGH!

GROOGH! TASTES LIKE NOTHING ON EARTH!

HERE! TAKE IT BACK, IT'S NOT FIT FOR A DOG!

HEY! LOOK AT THIS! BONES THIS TIME! I SUPPOSE THE MACHINE THOUGHT WE WANTED SOMETHING THAT WAS FIT FOR A DOG.

NOW, LISTEN! DO IT RIGHT THIS TIME. SEND US A BIG JAM TART—PLEASE—WITH CRISS-CROSS PASTRY ON IT.

OH, PLEASE—PLEASE!

YIPPEE! AT LAST WE'VE GOT WHAT WE ASKED FOR.

I WONDER IF IT'S BECAUSE WE SAID "PLEASE"?

IT MUST BE. ALWAYS REMEMBER TO SAY "PLEASE" AFTER THIS.

WE'RE GOING SHOPPING NOW—FOR FIREWOOD AND SUGAR!

HULLO! WHAT'S THIS THE GANG HAVE GOT?

PUT IN THE SUGAR AND FIREWOOD!

LOLLIPOPS, PLEASE!

SURE ENOUGH! SAYING "PLEASE" DOES THE TRICK! LOVELY LOLLIPOPS!

HOI! LOOK AT THAT.

HELP! HERE'S THE GASWORKS' GANG!

WE WANT COCONUT SNOWBALLS!

LOAD IT UP WITH COCONUTS AND SUGAR

THEY'VE GOT THEIR SNOWBALLS ALL RIGHT—GIANT ONES~ RIGHT IN THEIR UGLY DIALS!

HOWL!
OUCH!

HA! HA! HA! THEY SHOULD HAVE SAID "PLEASE".

THAT FINISHED THE GASWORKS GANG. I'VE AN IDEA—POUR IN FLOUR AND SAUSAGES!

HOT DOGS, PLEASE!

HOORAY! OUT COME HOT DOGS!

AND IN COMES THE DOUGH! THANK YOU! THREEPENCE EACH!

WEE DAVIE AND KING WILLIE

The pals from the palace in the principality of Pomegrania had seven series of adventures in The Beano between 1952 and 1957. This prime page is from 1957.

GR-R! THIS ZOO PROGRAMME IS A FLOP! ALL WE'VE SEEN IS ONE MANGY OLD HYENA. LET'S GO DOWN AND INVESTIGATE.

DOWN AT THE ZOO.

WHY ARE YOU ONLY SHOWING THAT HYENA?

THIS HYENA IS THE ONLY ANIMAL LEFT IN THE ZOO, SIRE! WE'VE HAD NO NEW STOCK FOR YEARS.

HYENA

SO ALONG AT THE TV STUDIO.

CUT THIS ZOO SHOW OFF, MR. PRODUCER. I'M GOING TO GIVE A TALK ON A BIG-GAME HUNTING EXPEDITION THAT I'M GOING TO MAKE TO RE-STOCK THE ZOO!

IN A FEW MINUTES WILLIE IS ON TV.

BLAH — BLAH! AND NOW I WOULD LIKE TO SHOW YOU SOME OF THE TRAPS THAT I'LL BE USING TO CATCH THE ANIMALS.

BUT OUTSIDE A JUNGLE TRADING-POST.

GOLLY! HEAR THAT? AN EXPEDITION TO CATCH WILD ANIMALS! QUICK! SPREAD THE NEWS AROUND THE JUNGLE!

THE BUSH TELEGRAPH IS WORKING.

LOOK OUT FOR HUNTERS!

ON THEIR WAY NOW!

GET OUT OF THE WAY QUICKLY!

TRAPS!

ZOO!

GENERAL ALERT!

SCRAM!

AND WHEN WILLIE ARRIVES IN THE WILDS.

WHERE ARE ALL THE ANIMALS? WE'VE BEEN HERE TWO DAYS AND HAVEN'T EVEN SEEN A GRASSHOPPER!

I CAN'T SEE ANYTHING MOVING AT ALL!

MEANWHILE IN THE POMEGRANIAN CAPITAL.

LET'S MAKE FOR THE PALACE!

IT'S AN INVASION!

WE'RE FAR SAFER HERE THAN WE WOULD BE IN THE JUNGLE!

IN THE ZOO.

WE'LL BE SAFE LOCKED IN HERE UNTIL THE ANIMALS GO AWAY!

KING WILLIE'S FILLED THE ZOO — BUT NOT WITH ANIMALS!

WILLIE RETURNS TO THE PALACE.

SO THIS IS WHERE THE ANIMALS HAVE GOT TO!

HYENA

HA-HA-HA!

HA-HA-HA!

ANY MORE BRIGHT IDEAS, SIRE?